The Deal

WITH

Dakota

also by
Michelle Dykman

Her Sanctuary, His Heart

You, Me, and the Stars
BETHEL PRIVATE SCHOOL SERIES | BOOK ONE

Someone Like You
BETHEL PRIVATE SCHOOL SERIES | BOOK TWO

You Found Me
BETHEL PRIVATE SCHOOL SERIES | BOOK THREE

If Only In My Dreams
A SNOWY SPRINGS ROMANCE | BOOK ONE

The Deal

WITH

Dakota

A SNOWY SPRINGS ROMANCE

MICHELLE DYKMAN

AMBASSADOR INTERNATIONAL
GREENVILLE, SOUTH CAROLINA & BELFAST, NORTHERN IRELAND
www.ambassador-international.com

The Deal with Dakota

©2023 by Michelle Dykman
All rights reserved

Paperback ISBN: 978-1-64960-426-2
eISBN: 978-1-64960-474-3
Library of Congress Control Number: 2023940359

Cover design by Hannah Linder Designs
Interior Typesetting by Dentelle Design
Edited by Katie Cruice Smith

Scripture taken from the Holy Bible, New International Version®, NIV® Copyright ©1973, 1978, 1984, 2011 by Biblica, Inc.® Used by permission. All rights reserved worldwide.

AMBASSADOR INTERNATIONAL
Emerald House Group, Incorporated
411 University Ridge, Suite B14
Greenville, SC 29601, USA
www.ambassador-international.com

AMBASSADOR BOOKS
The Mount
2 Woodstock Link
Belfast, BT6 8DD, Northern Ireland, UK
www.ambassadormedia.co.uk

The colophon is a trademark of Ambassador, a Christian publishing company.

For my parents, I didn't know how much love it took until I became a parent myself. Thank you.

To the team at Ambassador, thank you. Thank you for your support, encouragement, and feedback on each of my stories. This would not be possible without you. Thank you to my family for your love and understanding. And thank you to my Lord for this privilege of sharing Your hope to all of us in need of a Savior.

Above all, love each other deeply,
because love covers over a multitude of sins.

—1 Peter 4:8

Chapter One

Maybe this had been a mistake. Dakota Manning pushed the gear shift back into drive and pulled out from the parking bay. She had to leave; there was no other option. The painful beat of her heart drove her blood in a frenzy around her adrenaline-soaked body. She had to be quiet, and she had to move quickly. Bobby wouldn't like it, but right now, she didn't care what Bobby thought.

A shudder racked her body as Bobby's livid face invaded her mind—his cheeks flushed dark red and his dark eyes black with hatred. Another shudder. She never wanted to see those eyes again or have those calloused fists aimed at her.

A quiet sob pushed from her chest, and she quickly suppressed it. Bobby didn't like to see her cry; he said she was weak. The tears ran down uncontrollably, and all she could hear were the incessant laughter and insults that were hurled her way in her moments of weakness. Yet the tears continued; she could do nothing to stop them burning through the holes of her dignity. Bobby would be so angry when he found her gone. Maybe it was better she turn around before he found out; then, everything would be fine again. *No, it wouldn't, it never was.*

She took a deep, shuddering breath, wincing at the pain that radiated from the left side of her body—a bruise left over from another night. The pain cleared her mind and spurred her on with the choice she'd made. She would never return to that again. If she was careful and found a peaceful place to hole up, she'd be safe, and Bobby wouldn't be able to find her. *What if he did?*

Another tremor passed through her slight frame, and she winced again, wiping almost unconsciously at the small drops of blood leaking from the cut on her lip. Bobby had been angry the night before. Dakota had burned the dinner by accident. At first, Bobby had laughed; but as the brown bottles became more and more abundant on the dining room table, his laughter had turned to resentment and then to violence.

More tears and more blood. She gasped her tears back. She couldn't pull over and give into them now—not with Bobby still so close.

The quiet suburban roads gave way to the open emptiness of the freeway. Miles fled under her tires, distancing her further and further from the nightmare that had been her life for the past nine years. How had it come to this? She wiped her sleeve over her wet face and nose as her clunky sedan became one with the night. It was eerily quiet, except for the sudden burst of brightness from the lonely street lights and the odd passing car. Minutes passed into hours, and still, she drove. Quavering urgency pressed her to do so.

Another light appeared, closing in on her. Dakota's head thundered in time with her heart. Had he found her so soon? The large shadow came closer, forming the shape of a large truck. Dakota put her foot down flat, and the sedan lurched to answer. But the truck was faster, its engine bigger. Mile by mile, it caught up to her, eventually pulling even with her; and then, the large, black F-250 sped past her, the driver disappearing into the night without a second glance at Dakota.

Breath rushed out of her, and she inhaled deeply to steady it, almost losing her handle on the steering column in her relief. It wasn't Bobby. He hadn't found her.

Slowly, her foot eased off the gas pedal, bringing the car to a normal speed. Grimacing at her foolishness, Dakota pulled off at a nearby gas station. At the rate she was going, she wouldn't get out of the state before she ran out.

Ever vigilant, Dakota stepped out of the door, starting at every hoot or squeak she heard on her way into the small convenience store. She settled the cap lower on her head and slid the dark glasses she'd grabbed at the door over her face. Bobby wouldn't recognize her like this, she hoped.

Quickly concluding her business in the convenience store and the ladies' room, Dakota strolled casually back to the car, the tension in her back wrapping a tight band across her already labored chest. Bobby always knew where to hit so no marks would show until, of course, niceties didn't matter. They hadn't mattered for a long time.

She wiped quickly at the wetness gathering once again in her eyes. There would be time for tears later, time to find a way to live with the scars.

She flung the shopping bag into the passenger seat beside her on her way into the driver seat. The car grumbled loudly as she switched it on, and then she was on her way again, pushing past the city limits and into the open road where there was only her and the star-spangled night.

Night slowly gave way to morning as the first burst of sunrise flooded the sky with pale pinks, oranges, and purples. Her spirits lifted, temporarily overpowering the mind-numbing exhaustion that dragged her limbs. Blinking quickly, she refocused on the road, the two cans of energy drink and handful of chocolate bars she'd bought a thing of the past. And she desperately needed a ladies' room.

Sighing again, she took the last drink of water before tossing the bottle into the packed back seat. Her whole life was in those bags—well, what was left of it. The urgency became too strong, and she grudgingly pulled over at the nearest gas station. Harsh sunlight bounced off the white-covered field and mountains and blinded her as she climbed out of the car. Stunned for a moment, she forgot where she was going and stared in awe at the marvel around her.

"Can I help you?" a young voice asked from behind the gas tank.

Dakota came back to herself with a start and remembered where she was and why. "Uh, no thanks. I'm looking for the ladies' room," she said without turning.

Her cap and sunglasses lay where she'd left them on the passenger seat. She grabbed them and slipped her disguise back into place before walking over to the young man, her eyes trained on the floor.

"Ah, sure. It's around back," he said as she came nearer.

"Thank you," she whispered and changed direction. He'd forget her soon enough.

Thrusting her shoulders back and lifting her head high, she walked to the bathroom as if she didn't have a care in the world. There. That didn't look suspicious.

A few minutes later, she was on the road again, the young man long forgotten. She hoped he'd forget her just as easily. Maybe Bobby wouldn't come. She shook her head. No, he always made good on his threat, always.

Determination stiffened her spine, and she pressed her foot heavier on the gas pedal, fleetingly admiring the wide stretches of farmlands blurring past her and disappearing into the distance. The band around her chest inched open so that now she didn't feel like she was permanently inside a clamp but more like the shirt she wore was too tight.

The air suddenly filled with an incessant, high-pitched ringing and drowned out the soft hum of the car. Dakota cringed and grabbed the phone from her bag. Did Bobby know how to trace it? He'd always watched those late-night cop shows. He was always angry afterward, and he'd never tell her why.

The piercing ring continued as she glanced at the screen. Bobby. She could already hear the crude and cutting words that would follow. Not stopping to kill the call, she untangled her vice grip on the steering wheel to dismember her phone and hurl it into the nearest field. Her heart panged painfully as she watched it fly. It was the last gift she had from her mother and father, and now, even that was gone from her.

Dakota blinked quickly; sorries always came too late. That was a bridge she'd burned beyond repair a long time ago.

Another hour passed, and the exhaustion she'd hoped would be extinguished with her second wind became unbearable. Her head nodded, and she hurriedly flipped it back up and tightened her hands on the steering wheel again as the car swerved and missed a deep ditch on the side of the road. She needed rest, and she needed it in a hurry.

A bright red sign greeted her tired eyes: *Snowy Springs 100 miles.* Pushing forward, she continued to drive. Snowy Springs sounded like a nice, small town. Maybe it was like one of those shown in the movies that came on at Christmastime. It sounded like the perfect place to rest, and maybe, just maybe, she could stay there for a few days before moving on toward Denver.

Rejuvenated by the thought of sleep, Dakota pressed on and hoped that Snowy Springs would be just far enough for her to find some peace.

Chapter Two

The loud hum of the wood saw cooled the blood pumping angrily through Aaron's body. Of all the things that he could have found in the apartment above his shop, it had to be Lacey's sweater. As if the day hadn't started out bad enough.

First, Mrs. Sutherland called to say that she wasn't able to help out at the store anymore—something about her grandchildren needing their grandmother everyday across town. Then the transmission went out on his father's old truck. It had been ailing for a while, but he didn't think it was that serious until it had given up the ghost, thankfully right outside the shop. He called Al, the local mechanic, who would be around in a few hours.

And then, he'd gone upstairs to find a part he'd left there and found Lacey's sweater instead. The sight pierced him like a freshly sharpened spear impaling him to the wall. *Lord, this really isn't my idea of funny,* he silently fumed.

The saw continued to hum and then stopped with a thunderous crack. A thick, wooden board slanted across the table fell and split into a jagged diagonal line, one half on the floor and the other still laying on the work bench. Frustrated, Aaron slammed the switch off and flung his goggles back onto the workbench. He took a few ragged breaths. This was getting him nowhere.

After six torturous months, the apartment still reeked of her floral scent—a scent he'd loved on her and now hated. With one sweep of his hand, he brushed back his thick, sweaty hair. It probably needed to be cut again; he'd grown it out just to make Lacey angry.

Dust fell from his hands as he dusted the ever-present saw shavings from them. One of the things Lacey hated was the dust cloud that seemed to follow him wherever he went. It was a hazard of being in construction—one he'd never minded until its presence had been unceremoniously thrown in his face.

Aaron sighed out loud. What a fool he'd been.

"Aaron, Aaron, are you in here?"

A sudden pang hit his chest at the sound of his sister's voice as he thought of the earlier phone call he'd had with an old friend, Noah Thomas.

"Aaron, they found him; he's coming home," Noah had said, an edge of disbelieving apprehension in his voice.

"Michael? They found him?"

Noah hmmed in response. A lightness filled Aaron's chest. "When? Where? How?"

"We don't have any details yet, but I'll let you know as soon as I do."

With that, Noah had ended the call.

Aaron sighed. The incredulity of the conversation had yet to penetrate his brain. And then, there was Sarah. What would he tell her? Should he tell her? How would she react?

"In the back, Sarah."

His sister walked in, her long, hurried stride reaching him—a hazard, he guessed, of forever being in a hurry somewhere except if it involved a book.

"So, what brings you to my humble abode today?" he asked, accepting her gentle peck on the cheek. Would now be a good time to tell her?

Sarah frowned. "Where's Mrs. Sutherland? Is she sick?"

"No, she, uh . . . was needed elsewhere. She called and gave her notice this morning, very apologetic. I almost felt bad accepting that she was leaving me in the lurch."

"Oh dear," Sarah said. "How can I help?"

Aaron rubbed her head affectionately. "There's nothing you need to do, squirt. I'll take care of it. You have enough on your plate right now." No, he wouldn't tell her now. Not when she was finally beginning to heal.

"But . . . "

"Sarah . . . don't you have somewhere you need to be?"

"No, but I can see you're trying to get rid of me, so I'll just go. Did you want help cleaning the apartment?"

The acid in his chest burned his throat, and he swallowed it back. "Nah, I'll let you know when I've gotten rid of Lacey's stuff, and then you can have at it."

Sympathy swept over his sister's face, and she silently squeezed his hand. Lacey's betrayal had stung the whole family. Lacey and Avery had grown up together, and she'd practically lived at their house. So much for forever.

Sarah walked away, stopping to glance over her shoulder at the pink sweatshirt that lay in a crumpled heap on the wooden stairs. She picked it up and climbed the wooden stairs to the top. He heard the movement of boxes and the clap of footsteps on the upstairs floor. Sarah was probably cleaning.

He sighed again. As much as he hated to admit it, he was glad she'd taken the task off his hands. He didn't have the strength to face it today, not when so much else filled his thoughts. He lifted a second board onto the worktable and switched on the saw, carefully guiding the board between the guards so that the perfect two-by-four spat out the other side.

Michael. He couldn't believe his friend had been found. After three years. How had they found him? The better questions was how was he still alive? That thought caught like a rock in his throat. Michael was alive. Aaron swallowed hard. Thank You, God.

The wood wobbled under his hand. He guided it back in line. He continued the action until neat rows lined the workshop walls. He hoped they would have enough to get a start on the community center roof before the heavy snow set in.

The bell at the front of the store jingled, and Aaron carefully set his current board aside and wiped his hands on a nearby rag.

"How can we help?" he asked and came to a halt at the entrance of the workshop.

"It's just me. I've come by to collect the rest of the boxes," Sarah said.

"I didn't hear you leave."

"I thought it was best to leave you in your man cave. I didn't want to disturb you."

"Thanks," he said softly. It was days like today that he was glad for family. He only wished Michael was here; maybe he could help him make sense of the series of events over the last few months.

Sarah gazed at him sympathetically. "Whatever you need, you know I'm here." She retreated up the stairs.

A high stack of boxes preceded Sarah down the stairs a short while later. "That's the last of it," she said.

Aaron nodded and braced himself as the last remnants of his foolish dreams were ushered out the door by his sister. Oddly, the weight that had taken up residence in the middle of his chest on that fateful day eased slightly. But the pain remained lurking like a bandit in the dark recesses of his heart.

The door dinged again. "Sarah, I thought you were done."

"I'll admit I might be stronger but certainly not as pretty," Al said, closing the door firmly behind him.

Aaron grudgingly smiled. "Morning, Al. Good to see you. I'll tell Sarah."

A deep bellow echoed around the store. "No need. I told her myself on my way in." Al's gloves landed with a thud on the front counter of the hardware store as he moved his heavy girth between the shelves.

"The truck giving you problems? What's it this time?"

"The transmission."

A low whistle blew from between Al's teeth. "I think it's time you consider looking for a new truck." Al's hard features softened with compassion, and he placed a gentle hand on Aaron's shoulder. "Look, my boy, I know you miss your dad, but that truck needs to go."

"Not today, Al." Not when all his emotion felt like a bag of chips tossed into the air.

Al nodded his white head. "Okay, boy. I'll see what I can do, but I'm not making any promises."

"Thanks, Al." Aaron pulled the truck keys from his pocket and handed them to Al. He would look at the truck himself if he could find the time; but with the store, the community center, and the upcoming Christmas program, he barely had time to sleep.

Al let himself out of the store with his usual slow gait. Aaron grinned; old Al had been one of his father's best friends until he'd died.

He lifted the next sheet of board onto the work bench and got lost once again in the hum of the saw.

A few hours later, the phone rang, buzzing him back to reality.

"Aaron?"

"Aaron, it's Al. I need a hand. There's a car that ran off the road. Can you meet me at the corner of Fifth and Second just outside town?"

"Sure, I'll get Mom to lend me her truck and be there in twenty." He ended the call and hurried to his mother's store next door to his.

"Mom, I need to borrow your truck."

"Well, hello to you, too."

Aaron smiled sheepishly. "Sorry." He kissed his mother on her cheek. "Al needs my help with a car that ran off the road at Fifth and Second."

"Where's your father's truck?" she asked and looked up from behind the tall counter where the checkout was.

"Transmission gave out. Don't worry. Al will have it fixed in no time."

His mother handed over the keys, and he kissed her again and hurried out the door. "Thanks. Watch the shop for me please." He paused. "When I'm done, can we talk?"

"Sure." His mother's brow bent in worry.

"It's good news. I promise."

"Okay, see you later then."

"Thanks, Mom."

The truck sprang to life as he turned the key and pulled off toward Fifth Street. Al stood beside a compact, light blue sedan. The driver had managed to nose-dive into the rain ditch on the side of the road. Aaron wasn't surprised; the roads had been slippery last night. And judging by the baldness of the small tires, they hadn't stood a chance against the icy tar.

"Drunk?" he asked Al as he came to stand beside him.

"No, I think she was just tired. Ambulance took her to Snowy Med just under an hour ago."

"Okay, what do you need me to do?"

Al handed Aaron a long winch strap and iron hook. "See if you can jam that under the rear axle, and I'm going to try to pull her out."

Icy cold wet his jacket as Aaron slid his tall body under the small car. *Who drives something like this? The owner must be tiny to fit in a car this small.*

"Okay, I think I have it," he said and wiggled his way back out onto the shoulder.

A loud whine filled the air; and the long, thick cable became taut and, with unyielding force, lifted the small car from the muddy hole. It landed with a hard thud behind Al's tow truck.

Al made a quick circle around the car and truck. "Looks like I'm in for a busy week."

"Did the driver have anyone with her?"

"Nah, just her. She was unconscious, and I didn't recognize her. Must be from out of town."

"Do you think she knows anyone?"

Al sighed. "I don't know."

Pity squeezed Aaron's chest. He knew tons about being alone. A gentle nudge moved him into action.

"Al, lower the car down for a minute. I'm gonna grab a few of the bags and take them to the hospital. I'm sure whoever was in this car could use them."

A proud smile appeared on Al's weathered face. "That's mighty kind of you, boy."

"Yeah, yeah," Aaron said gruffly.

After grabbing two of the larger bags from the back seat of the tiny car, Aaron drove toward Snowy Med.

Chapter Three

Why did she hurt everywhere? And what was that beep, beep that chimed in time with her heart? Instantly alert, she sat up and winced at the pain that lanced through her body.

"Easy there, miss; you've taken a bad knock," a placid female voice said beside her.

Eyes wide, heart racing, Dakota looked around the room. Where was she? Plain, white walls and linen, along with a large array of machinery, surrounded her. She was in a hospital. Had Bobby brought her? She needed to leave before he returned. How had he found her so quickly?

A tall, dark-skinned woman came into view. "Can you tell me your name?" she asked in a pleasantly soothing voice.

"Is Bobby here?" Dakota asked, desperation bleeding into her words. The lady beside her smiled kindly. "No, there is no Bobby here. I can call him for you if you want."

Bittersweet relief made her body limp. "No, no need. My name's Dakota Manning."

"Okay, Dakota, where are you from?"

"Oklahoma." Dakota flopped back down onto the hard bed, exhausted, while the nurse scribbled something on her clipboard.

"Do you know where you are, Dakota?"

"In a hospital? I was heading toward a town called Snowy Springs and... How did I get here?" Her heart, which had been quietly settling down from the fear of seeing Bobby, leaped into action at full speed again. The machine beside her chimed loudly, and a flashing red light flickered on and off.

The nurse gently patted Dakota's hand. "It's all right," she said in a soft, reassuring voice, like her mother used to use when she was frightened. "You're in Snowy Med hospital in Snowy Springs. I believe your car ran off the road just inside the town boundaries. Had you been drinking?"

She'd made it. "No, I think I fell asleep."

"Long journey?"

"The longest." It had taken years for her to build up the courage to leave Bobby, to leave the confines of his control and be on her own. She'd tried to change him, show him a better way. She shouldn't have wasted her time. Bobby would not change for anything.

The nurse seemed to understand something and tilted her head kindly. "Welcome to Snowy Springs, Dakota. I hope you'll enjoy our town. No better place to spend the holidays."

A small smile cracked Dakota's dry lips and slowly stretched over her mouth. When was the last time she'd smiled? "Thank you."

"I'll leave you to get some rest. The doctor will be around soon." The nurse took notes at each machine she stopped at and then at a large, gray file at the foot of Dakota's bed.

"Sorry, I didn't get your name," Dakota said.

"I'm Ebony. If you need anything, let me know, okay?" Ebony rested her hand on Dakota's ankle. "Rest now. You look like you could use it."

Dakota rearranged the thin sheet and thick, gray, weaver-stitch blanket around her body and let herself sleep.

What seemed like minutes later, there was a loud rap on the door. Hollow fear snaked its way through her. She sat up and braced herself for the wrath that was waiting outside that door.

Her breath locked in her chest as the door slowly opened to reveal a man—but not the one she'd been expecting. Instead, there was a tall, dark-haired man with wide shoulders, a trim waist, and deep brown eyes that caused a flutter in her stomach as they met hers. His arms looked like how she remembered her father's— strong and tapered with muscle. This man knew what hard work looked like.

Another sliver of fear slid up her spine. It was then that she really took notice of his eyes; they didn't look too threatening, but one could never be too careful.

"Are you lost?" she asked, gasping a shaky breath.

"Sorry, I don't suppose you know who I am." The man closed the door and took a step closer to the bed. Fear skittered up her spine. Had Bobby sent him to get her?

"Stop!" she screamed. "Who are you?"

The man's face twisted into a deep frown; weariness filled his handsome face. "Okay, maybe I should get someone else to do this." He held out two large bags for her to see. "These yours?" he asked.

A wave of something clean and spicy tickled her nose at the movement.

For a moment, Dakota stared blankly at the suitcases. "Where did you get those?" she demanded.

"From a tiny-sized car that no decent human being should be driving in this weather." His voice was rough like he was annoyed for some reason.

Dakota grimaced. "Was it light blue?" she asked.

"Yes, and with tires as bald as my uncle Tom—if I had one," he said. A casual smile lifted his check, and he placed the bags on the floor nearer to the bed. He stepped back toward the door and leaned back against it, studying her. What did he see?

"Yes, well, I wasn't prepared. It doesn't really snow heavily where I come from."

The man nodded; his scrutiny was unnerving. An uncomfortable silence descended on the room, broken only by the crackle of her starchy sheet clenched between her fists.

"I suppose I should introduce myself. I'm Aaron Bakker. I own a hardware store in town. Al and I pulled that excuse-for-a-car out of the ditch."

His voice had a warm quality, with a soft cadence of the South. Bobby's voice had been deep like rusted metal that pitched higher when he was mad.

"Dakota Manning, owner of excuse-for-a-car and just stopping through on my way to Denver. Who is Al?"

"It's nice to meet you, Dakota. Is there someone I can call, let them know you're okay?" He pressed off the door. "Al is the town mechanic and the one who pulled your death trap from the ditch."

Shame bowed her head, and she swallowed back the emotion gathered in her chest. "Oh. And no, no one who matters."

"I'm sorry to hear that," Aaron said. His voice gentle, kind. She was sure his kindness was a figment of her imagination. Men weren't nice to woman like her.

He moved again. She lifted her head to look at him. Aaron stood slightly closer to the bed. "I'll let you get some rest then." His dark eyes were so much like Bobby's and yet so different. Understanding, like he had compassion for her. *Wishful thinking, Dakota.*

The door opened and closed with a soft snick, and she closed her eyes again into a restful sleep.

Aaron let out a deep breath as the white door closed quietly behind him, startled for a moment that he had to catch his breath. The fear that swam in the light eyes of the woman occupying the room cut him to the quick. What had happened to someone for them to be that afraid of another human being? Why did it bother him so much?

Perhaps it was her fine, almost pixie-like features and the soft, blonde hair that swept along her shoulders. She looked tiny, wrapped up in those white sheets, her arms clenched over her stomach, and damaged like that death trap she called a car.

An overpowering wave of protectiveness had crashed over him as soon as those wide, winter gray eyes had clashed with his. He'd seen the fading bruises along her uncovered arms and wondered about their origin. Grimacing, he walked away. It was probably that she reminded him of Lacey, and look where that had gotten him. Cursing quietly, he whipped his phone out and dialed Al's number.

"Hey, Al, did you make it back to the shop yet?"

"Yeah, how's the driver?"

"She's fine. I think a bit shell-shocked, but she looks okay."

"I did some digging round town, and no one knows anything about this girl."

"I'm not surprised. She says she's just passing through."

Al grunted. "She won't be going anywhere in a hurry; that little dime of a car is pretty broken."

"Yeah, like its owner," he muttered.

"What's that, son?" Al interjected.

"Ah, nothing. How long is the truck's transmission going to take?"

Al counted quietly. "Long—about two weeks to have that tin can up and running again. I can give you the loner if you want."

Aaron shuddered at the thought of Al's loner. It was a huge, green pickup that was probably older than he and Sarah combined, but what choice did he have? Mom needed her truck back. "Sure. I'll be right there to come get it."

He ended the call with Al and turned to glance at the door at the end of the hall again. *It's not your problem, Aaron.* Dakota had managed to get herself this far; she could get herself to wherever she was going.

Concluding that he'd done his Good Samaritan work for the day, Aaron headed back to his mother's truck. He'd go to his mother's store, then to Al's, and then back to the shop. A pile of lumber awaited his attention.

A light, clean smell of something sweet and tart like raspberries filled his nose as he climbed into the cab. He'd noticed that first when he'd placed Dakota's bags beside him in the truck. It suited her. The smell matched her soft, pink mouth. *Really, Aaron?*

The muddy stench from the ice-filled trenches along the road hadn't permeated the bags. Mom would be glad. He didn't fancy the idea of hearing about how dirty her truck seats were for the next six months. The truck drove as if it had a brain of its own, turning down the familiar street and back to the hardware store as he passed under the dying light of the setting sun, unable to dismiss the vision of the small, frightened woman with heather eyes.

He brought the truck to a halt outside his shop; a yellow light still burned in the bookstore next door. Sarah was probably taking inventory again. That girl worked too hard. Without complaint, she kept their family going after all they'd been through in the last three years. The bookstore door opened with a familiar whistling trill, and Sarah came around the corner, a dirt smudge on her left cheek.

"Working late?" he asked.

Sarah sighed. "Yeah, another shipment of cozy mystery novels came in, and Mom's arthritis is acting up. She went home hours ago."

Aaron's heart panged with regret. Where would they be without his sister? He needed to tell her the news he'd received earlier, but first, he needed to talk to his mom. "You do too much, kid." He kissed her head. "And again, I need your help."

"Your truck?" She smiled teasingly.

"Yeah, Al's giving me his loner until he can fix it."

Sarah shuddered dramatically and let out a happy giggle. "Well, lucky you."

"Thanks, can you give me a lift?"

"Sure. Let me lock up the shop, and then I can take you. I'll collect Mom in the morning, so don't worry about the truck."

"I'll meet you outside."

After they'd collected the truck and Sarah had left their mother's house, Aaron made coffee, then went to sit beside his mother on the long, paisley sofa. A fire cracked and popped softly in the fireplace, its warmth reaching his frozen hands.

"What is it, Aaron?" his mother asked gently, laying a hand on his wrist.

"They found him, Mom. Michael—they found him. He's alive."

His mother gasped, her fingers trembling where they met his skin. "When? Where? Oh, Aaron," she said. Tears filled her voice.

He looped his arm over her shoulder and drew her into his chest. "I know, Mom," he said, emotion muffling his voice. "I know." Tonight, they would rejoice. In the morning, he would figure out how to tell his sister.

Chapter Four

"Well, Dakota, everything looks good. We can discharge you bright and early tomorrow."

"Discharge?" Dakota asked quickly and stared wide-eyed at Dr. Swanson's face. The night had been a restless one, and she'd welcomed the medication the night nurse had given her to help her sleep. Aside from a slight throb in her head, she felt better.

"Yes, your vitals are good, and there aren't any adverse effects from that knock to your head. I would think you'd be raring to get out of here."

"Ah, yeah, sure," she said as her chest rattled with anxiety.

What had seemed like the best plan suddenly filled her with uncertainty. *You had to leave, Dakota.* Yes, she did, but what would she do now? Her plans to get a hotel for the night and then drive on to Denver suddenly seemed impossible.

"I'll see that the paperwork is ready when you are."

"Thank you."

Ebony walked in as the doctor exited. "Morning, Dakota. How are you feeling today?"

"According to Dr. Swanson, I'm doing well," she said with forced cheeriness. The rough, cotton sheets twisted busily between her fingers as she tried hard to take no notice of her wildly racing heart. As had been the case, Ebony's watchfulness didn't miss a thing.

"Trouble?" Ebony asked as she walked around the room and checked the machines.

"You wouldn't happen to know a place where I could stay for a few days, would you?"

A frown dipped Ebony's brow, and she tapped her cheek. "It'll be pretty tough at this time of year. Almost everything is sold out because of the town's Christmas festival. I'll keep an ear out today and let you know if I hear of anything."

"Thanks," Dakota said and stretched her arms as high as she could above her head, smothering a loud groan. The pain in her side had lessened considerably with a bit of rest; the bruises on her ribs and shoulder, that had nothing to do with the crash, were better; and the dizziness was all but gone. Ebony checked her blood pressure and then removed the saline drip from her arm. "There. Dr Swanson will be around first thing in the morning to give you your discharge papers."

"Thank you for everything," she said. She'd felt more welcome in this place in one night than she had in a long time anywhere else.

"That's just Snowy Springs for you," Ebony said with a smile.

The door opened with a loud bang. A warm rush of air from the hallway preceded Aaron's bulky form.

"Sorry to barge in like this," he said. And then, as if only just noticing them, he said, "Morning, Ebony, Dakota. Doc told me you were awake."

Ebony covered a small smile with her hand and glanced at Dakota. "Ah, Aaron—just the person I need to see. Are you still looking to rent out that apartment above your shop?"

"Yeah, should be ready today. I put an ad in the paper. Bill said he'd run it this week."

"Perfect. Dakota here is looking for a place to stay, and with the Christmas festival . . . "

"All the inns in town are full," Aaron finished for her.

"Look, I don't think . . . " Dakota interrupted, but no one took notice of her. They seemed oblivious to the discomfort that wormed in her stomach. She didn't need help from anyone, least of all the giant of the man who scared the tar out of her.

"Sure, I'd be happy to rent it to Dakota," Aaron said.

His large frame came closer, and she reflexively folded her arms around her body to protect herself. Aaron glanced down at her then and stopped dead. His jovial expression was replaced with caution. "If that's okay with Dakota, that is," he said softly like he was soothing a scared child or animal.

How had he known she was afraid? Was it something she had done? Usually, she was really good at disguising her fear, but maybe it was Ebony's presence that put her more at ease. Whatever it was, it probably wasn't good. She hated feeling weak.

"I would need it for only a night or two," she said, carefully unfolding her arms and straightening her spine. Or maybe longer depending on the damage to her car.

"Great. Then, that's settled," Ebony said and clicked her flipchart closed. "I'll be right back."

Aaron lounged his frame against a nearby wall and watched her.

"Is there a reason you barged like a bull into my room?" she asked. Her words lacked the fire she'd hoped to add to them.

A grin quirked his lips. Lips—oh, he did have nice lips. Dakota squeezed her eyelids together. What did she think she was doing admiring this man?

"I just came from Al, the mechanic. He asked what you wanted to do with the stuff in your car. I said I would ask, seeing as I was on my way to one of my suppliers on this side of town."

"You couldn't just have called or something?" she asked, immediately knowing her question was a dumb one.

"I don't have your number," Aaron said and held up his phone teasingly.

Dakota's cheeks flushed; she'd walked right into that one.

"Ah yes. Even if you did, it wouldn't have helped. I lost my phone on the way into town."

Aaron's eyebrow raised above his head like he knew she'd thrown it out the window in a desperate effort to make sure Bobby couldn't find her. The blankets rattled under her hands, and she stilled them with one fierce movement.

"Anyway, he says your car isn't too badly damaged, just a few kinks in the fenders and mud in the engine. He should have it cleaned out in no time."

Another strike of anxiety hit her; the damage to her car would cost money to fix, and money was in desperately short supply.

"Does he have to fix it?" she asked through the tightness in her chest. Fear and anxiety mixed into a potent mess of nausea that crept up into her throat.

"If you want it to run."

Aaron pushed himself up from the wall and took a small step closer to the bed. "What's the matter?" he asked.

Dakota startled and looked up. The careful curiosity in his gaze robbed the air from her lungs. "I . . . uh . . . I . . . uh. I'm not sure how I'm going to pay for the repairs," she finished, her head bowed under the weight of her embarrassment.

A deep chuckle tickled her ears, and red-hot fury steamed into her. "I hardly think that's something to be amused about," she spat at him, overcome with the unfair turn her life had taken. Was this all there was to life—tough breaks and problems? When would she ever get a break and just be happy?

A memory of her mother's smiling face came forward, and a pang of longing squeezed Dakota's heart. She'd been happy at home—well, mostly. The reasons she'd left seemed so trivial. It had taken years for her to realize that while her parents grieved Kenny's death, they hadn't abandoned her. Boy, if they could see her now, they would be so disappointed.

"Dakota?" Was that kindness she heard? Why was this man being kind to her? She didn't deserve it. Bobby had told her often enough that men weren't kind to women like her.

"What?" she asked and then carefully softened her tone. "Sorry. Look, I'm really tired. Is there something else you need?"

Aaron sighed. "Listen, I wasn't laughing at your misfortune. I was laughing at my crazy thoughts. I'll make you a deal. I need someone to help me at the store, and you need a way to make money for the repairs."

"I won't be staying in town, Aaron." Why would he offer her a job—someone he barely knew? She'd probably screw it up. Better that she just get herself and stuff together and get out of town as soon as possible.

"I know, but any help I can find right now would be great. I have projects coming out of my ears, and I simply don't have the time to run the store and fix the community center. You would be doing me a favor if you accept—at least for as long as you're in town."

The genuine plea in his expression softened her innate reluctance to have anything to do with this man. She wanted to help, and she would; but she would ignore those soft brown eyes and the way they made her heart beat a little faster.

"I accept. And thank you."

"No, thank you. You're helping me out of a real bind. I'll call my sister, Sarah, and ask her to check on the apartment. When do you think you'll be ready to start?"

"I, ah, tomorrow. What exactly will I be doing? And what does it pay?"

"We can go over the details tomorrow when you're out. Either Sarah or I can collect you. Just tell Doc to give me a call, and I'll arrange for someone to come get you."

His words whirled around her head. Come get her? Just call? "Wait, what did you say?"

"Just ask the doc to call me, and I'll arrange for someone to come get you and take you to the store. The apartment is above my store." Aaron said the words slowly like she was mentally incapable of understanding a full sentence. Maybe the knock to her head had been worse than she'd anticipated. Nonsense. It was the fact that his words didn't make a lick of sense to her.

"Why would you do that?"

"Do what? Help?"

Dakota nodded.

The smile was back. "People in this town always look out for each other."

An unfamiliar gratitude swept over her, and wetness gathered at the corners of her eyes. She swallowed hard, drawn again to her clenched hands. "But I'm not from your town." She wasn't part of anyone or anything. She was alone, like an animal ostracized from its herd.

Warm fingers gently lifted her chin up to eyes the color of melted chocolate. His clean scent filled her senses. "That doesn't mean anything."

As if burned by the same spark that fizzled up her cheeks, he cleared his throat and dropped his hand. "You've been in town more than twenty-four hours, and that makes you one of us."

For some reason, she started to cry.

Chapter Five

"Hey, hey, I'm sorry. I didn't mean to upset you," he said and took another step closer. He stopped himself just before he reached out to her. What was going on with him?

The sadness and confusion that bled from every part of the woman before him punched Aaron low in the gut. What amazed him was the level of distrust and fear he saw in her eyes. Who had made her feel this way? And why was she so afraid?

"I'm sorry. If I said something to hurt you, I apologize."

Dakota continued to cry, shaking her head. He stood helpless beside her, unsure of what to do to help. Eventually, her tears ebbed. She reached for a box of tissues on the bedside table to wipe her eyes.

"Sorry," she whispered, curling into herself. Afraid, he could only guess of what.

"That's okay. Want to tell me how I can help?"

She shook her head again. "No." Her lips were pressed in a thin line; she wouldn't say anything further.

"I guess I'll be going then."

"Are you sure about offering me a job and a place to stay?"

"Of course," he said. And before he said something stupid again, he reached for the door handle.

Ruffling his hand through his already messy hair, he let himself out of the room. The gray hospital hallways were quieter than usual. The wide reception desk at the end of the hall came into view quickly, but with his long strides, it wasn't anything new.

Maybe the fact that he was so much bigger than she made her afraid of him. But how could that be? She hadn't been standing once when he'd seen her. So, what was it then? And the protectiveness he felt each time her misty gray eyes met his was unexplainable. He'd only just met the woman, and the idea of her being afraid of him vexed him to no end.

Why did it bother him so much that she was afraid of him? They didn't know each other from Adam. And why had he let himself be badgered by Ebony into giving her a place to stay and then offered her a job? None of it made sense to him.

Groaning under his breath, he dismissed his confusion. "Is Mabel here today?" he asked Ebony, who was working at the desk. Ebony lay down the chart she'd been working on and shook her head. "I can give her a message if you like."

"Can you ask her to please give me a call when Dakota is discharged tomorrow?"

Ebony arched her eyebrow. "I can do that. It's nice that you're helping her out. She seems a little lost."

"Yeah," he said with a heavy sigh. "Anyway, please give me a call— or Sarah, if I don't answer."

"Sure, will do."

A light shower of flurries fell as Aaron slid his truck into drive. The roads had been cleared earlier from the previous night's snowfall, and large heaps of salt-drenched ice lay against the curb.

His mind kept on drifting back and forth between his conversation with Dakota and finding the right time to tell his sister the news of Michael's return. More questions were ringing but no answers coming. Why had he agreed to help her? He had always been a help-out kind of guy; his parents had raised him to be that way. But this was a complete stranger he'd irrationally invited into his house. Okay, maybe not his house but as good as his. After all, the apartment was his, too. And what did he know of her credentials? For all he knew, she could rob him blind. But there was something that told him Dakota wasn't that kind of person. No, she was someone who was in desperate need of good, old fashioned Christian charity.

A large barn-like building came into view. The community center had been the focal point of any activity in Snowy Springs for as long as Aaron could remember. Between the bad weather and age, it had fallen in a week ago; no one had really been surprised, and the town council had immediately called him in to help.

Not that he minded construction. It was his work, and he loved what he did. But with a shortage of lumber and a fire that had all but wiped out the mill two towns over, he was struggling to get the project completed. Well, now, at least, he had someone to help him out at the store. Maybe Dakota's coming to Snowy Springs was Providential after all.

He rubbed his chin, still unsure what had possessed him to offer Dakota a job. It was clear she was running from something. No one packed up their life in their car and drove with no particular destination in mind without a reason. The question remained: what was she running from? Another question to which he had no answer.

And the even better one was would she answer if he asked? Probably not. She'd hightail it again.

Ripping his woolen hat from his head, he threw it on the work counter in the far left room and shrugged off his coat, eager to work off some of the tension in his body. Various groups of people busily worked around the community center. In the corner of the main hall, Aaron saw Sarah. He should probably give her the heads up about Dakota, or he'd be teased relentlessly.

You need to tell her about Michael. He knew he should, but he couldn't bear the look of hope that would no doubt bloom within her. What if Michael was nothing like they remembered? War was a terrible thing. He'd heard so many stories of soldiers returning different from when they'd left. What if Sarah got hurt again?

"Sarah," he called, hurrying over to her. Sarah smiled and said something to her companion before meeting him halfway.

"Where have you been?" she asked. "Mom told me you called hours ago to say you were on your way; and I get here, and you are nowhere to be found."

"Hey, easy there, squirt. I went to Al to check on the truck, and then I was at the hospital."

"Hospital? Are you sick?"

It hurt him to see the fear in his sister's eyes. Since Michael had disappeared and their father had passed, Sarah seemed to be in a constant state of stress over everyone's health. See, another good reason to let the news of Michael's return stay a secret until it needed to be told. "No, you know I went to help Al with a car yesterday?"

"Yes."

"Well, it was a young woman. Her name's Dakota." Sarah tilted her head sideways, a grin sliding up her cheek. "Stop right there. She needed help, and I offered."

"Okay, and what type of help are we talking?" She crossed her arms over her chest, amusement dancing across her face.

"She's renting the apartment, and I offered her a job."

Sarah's eyebrows disappeared into her hairline. "You offered her a job. Aaron, what . . . "

"I needed the help—you know that—and especially with the holiday season . . . " He shrugged, suddenly unsure if he'd made the right decision after all.

"That's nice of you, Aaron," she said at last.

"That's kind of what I need to talk to you about," he said hesitantly. "Dakota is being discharged tomorrow, and I need someone to pick her up if I'm not available and . . . "

"You want me to. That's fine, I'd be happy to help."

"Oh, and if you have a minute, would you mind getting some groceries for the apartment?"

"You're taking advantage of my generous nature, brother," Sarah teased. "But don't worry about it. If I can't, I'll ask Avery. I know you're busy."

"Thanks, I owe you one."

"Now, you owe me two, but who's counting?"

Aaron nodded with a wry grin.

"Now, I need to get back to the decorating committee meeting." Sarah climbed cautiously over some logs he and his men had yet to move from the pile of roof dumped in the middle and disappeared into one of the other rooms.

Blowing out a deep breath, Aaron hooked one half of a roof frame over his shoulder and made himself get back to work. There were only so many days left until Christmas Eve.

His mind quickly slid into the familiar pattern—nail, hammer, new board, nail, hammer, new board. The rhythm was familiar and required all his attention so that his mind couldn't drift once again to Dakota.

When his phone buzzed loudly in his pocket a few hours later, the sun had set, and the dark night sky could be seen through the community center windows.

"Yes?" he answered.

"Aaron, are you still coming today to get the rest of that lady's things?"

"Ah, yeah. Sorry, Al. I lost track of time. I'll be there in twenty."

"You're a good kid, Aaron."

He'd heard those words often from his dad and Al many times in past years. But for some reason, today, they caused a knot to form in his chest. He hoped he could live up to the expectation his father had always had of him.

"Thanks, Al. I'll see you in a bit."

"Thanks."

Whoever had invented the shower had her undying gratitude, Dakota thought as she rubbed the rough blue towel against her skin. After two days in the hospital, she'd been in desperate need of a good soaking. The hot water sluiced away the grime from driving and laying about in bed and left her alert and refreshed. Ebony had found her a small bottle of orange-scented soap and shampoo combination at the gift shop, and it was just what she needed. She would be forever grateful for Ebony's kindness.

Wringing the water from her sodden hair, she wrapped the smaller towel around it and quickly slipped on her favorite pair of sweats, pausing to study the bruises on her legs. They were fading, slowly. Hopefully these were the last she would ever have to hide. She grimaced at the smoke stench that still lingered on her clothes, even though she'd laundered before she'd left. She hoped this apartment would have a washer she could use. Or maybe Aaron knew of a laundromat nearby.

Aaron. Her stomach flipped over. He seemed like a really nice guy—way too nice for a girl like her.

Sighing softly, she began to repack her duffel. The putrid stench of Bobby's aftershave blew past her between her jeans and pajamas. The smell brought with it a wave of fear. She swallowed hard, fighting against the tide. It would be okay. She would be okay. She didn't let herself dwell on the huge mistake it was to take off with him all those years ago nor the things she'd done while there. She'd learned her lesson.

A small path of bruises on her hip caught her eye as she slid on her bright pink t-shirt. She'd learned it the hard way, just like Mama had always said. Dakota swallowed back the lump in her throat. Her mama had been right about Bobby. She'd seen what Dakota had refused to. Oh, how she missed her parents. Were they well? Did they think of her? What about her father? Was his heart still troubling him?

Storing the sweet memories of her parents for her dreams, Dakota readied her bags, looking forward to tomorrow. The feeling was both strange and frightening. It had been so long since she'd looked forward to anything. She clicked off the bed lamp, and the room sank into darkness. Dakota lay down and was out like a light.

Chapter Six

"And here we are." Aaron leaned back against the store's glass door and allowed Dakota to pass in front of him. The sweet smell of oranges followed her, and he inhaled deeply, drawn to the smell for an unexplainable reason. She smelled so good. The acrid smell of cigarettes that had surrounded her luggage was gone. Her scent was clean and womanly, stirring his blood.

Dakota stopped. Her head swung to the left and right before she turned to him. "I'm not sleeping in here, am I?" she asked. He knew what she saw. Aisles and aisles of tools, lumber, garden accessories, and machinery. To the right of them, a cash register sat on a long, boxy counter.

Her voice was small, almost childlike. He ruefully shook his head, unable to stop the grin that lifted his mouth. "No, just up the stairs," he said and gestured to the flight of stairs directly behind her.

The trip from the hospital had been filled with stilted conversation and large patches of silence. Dakota had sat stiff as a board beside him, her fingers endlessly worrying the hem of her pale pink sweatshirt. How he'd wished she'd just relax for a moment.

Pink seeped into Dakota's cheeks, and she was once again fascinated by her hands. She did that a lot, he'd come to realize, when she was uncomfortable.

"This way," he said and headed for the stairs, determined not to prolong the awkwardness between them. Dakota followed at a slower pace, leaving an expanse of distance between them. He listened for the hesitant trod of her shoes over the wooden floors of the store and the slight creaks as she climbed the stairs. When they reached the top, Aaron slung her duffel onto one of the newish black, square sofas, grateful to see grocery bags resting on the centre table of the kitchenette. He didn't want to be too presumptuous and put it in the bedroom; this was the safer option.

Dakota, still ill at ease, danced nervously from one foot to the other, her hands clenched into each other. He stayed the desire to walk over and soothe the rough redness of her fingers and again squashed the impulse to hug her. She looked like she could use one.

"Are those my things?" she asked, pointing to the pile of boxes in the middle of the room. Her body practically hummed with restlessness and fear as she ran her fingers up and down the rough linen of the sofa. It chaffed at him that she was so afraid.

"Yes." He paused unable to stop the urge to say something to her to make her feel more comfortable in his presence. "Dakota, I don't know what happened to you or who hurt you, but I'm not going to. You are safe here." Why he'd said those words, he'd never know; but the effect on her was instantaneous.

Dakota's cheeks stained with red, and she swallowed hard. Her gray eyes flicked to his and then around the room again before she reluctantly nodded. The tightness in her shoulders seemed to relax, if only a little.

Tension eased from him like the air from a balloon. "The bedroom is back down the hall; the bathroom is across the hall. There is a door between the apartment and the shop; so, if you need privacy, you can just close it, and I won't bother you."

"Okay," she said, so low he could barely make it out.

"There's food in the refrigerator, and if you don't feel like cooking, there is a pizza restaurant down the road."

At last, a glimmer of life entered her expression. "Aaron, this is too much. How on earth am I going to pay you back for all this? The place, the food, everything?"

"What time can you start tomorrow?" he asked with mock gravity, deliberately arranging his face into a pleasant smile.

Dakota chuckled. "What time does the store open?"

"I usually open at seven a.m., and I'm here until about nine. That's when I leave for the community center. My guys are fixing the roof; it caved in two weeks ago, and we need to get it fixed in time for the Christmas pageant. Four months might seem like a long time. However, the damage is so extensive, we need every moment."

He was rambling, something he never did. What was it about her that made his mind slip away from him? Heat crawled up his neck, and he roughly cleared his throat. "So, how about nine a.m.?"

"That's fine, and I don't know how to thank you. You and the whole town have been so kind to me." It still stunned him that she was so ridiculously grateful. Did no one outside of Snowy Springs help each other anymore?

"Like I said, you're welcome here." Before he said anything else stupid, he headed back down the stairs to collect the rest of Dakota's bags from the car.

On his last trip up, he heard the slow tread of footsteps up and down the floor of the apartment. She was as skittish as a newborn colt around him; maybe he should have asked Sarah to come instead. Dakota seemed to be more comfortable as long as there was another female present.

Oh well, it couldn't be helped. Taking the last two steps in one, he placed the boxes on the floor. "That's the last of it," he said.

Dakota came into the living room, a small pile of clothes balanced on her hands. "Thank you. Is there a washer or laundromat nearby? These clothes really need a good wash."

"You can use the washer at my house if you want. It's just down the street."

Rosy color drained from Dakota's cheeks. Oh dear, he'd said something wrong.

"N-n-no thanks. I'm sure I can find a laundromat somewhere in this town."

So, it was going to be like that. "In that case, Mrs. Bouwer owns the laundromat next door to the bakery. They're open until four."

"Thank you."

"You're welcome." He wished there was some way he could get her to understand that he meant it.

A wave of relief swept over her when Aaron finally said goodbye. The last few hours of nervous tension had rattled her. Hard wood pressed into her arm as she rested her shoulder on her window frame and admired the bright Christmas lights that punctuated the shadows of the street below. This town was truly beautiful, and the people were unlike any others she'd ever met. Her parents would feel right at home in a place like this.

The familiar pang echoed into her heart. Oddly, it was met with another emotion that felt like hope. Now that she was free of Bobby, maybe she could make peace with her parents. She quickly squashed the thought. Her parents would never forgive her. And how could she ever face them with the knowledge of what she'd done?

Lights burned in the store next door and shadowed a young couple smiling and walking happily down Main Street. The gentle sound of Christmas chorales played somewhere in the night, and Dakota bent her head closer to the window to catch a glimpse of where. She couldn't see anything more than a few stores and the open night sky.

Aaron walked below, no doubt on his way from the bookstore next door. She quickly leaned out of sight, slightly breathless. There was something about that man that confused her. Why was it that each time he was near her, a feeling of safety would cover her like a warm blanket? Her pulse sped up, and all the reservations she had about men seemed to not matter.

Chiding herself for being silly, she went to inspect the fridge. With a bit of persuasion, the fridge door swung open, and Dakota's stomach rumbled loudly at the sight of so much good food. Moisture welled in her eyes, and if her relationship with God still mattered to her, she'd thank Him for good people like the Bakkers and Ebony and Mabel from the hospital for welcoming her into their town.

But God was long gone with her parents. The morbid tenor of her thoughts pressed her into action, and in a short while, the smell of bacon and eggs permeated the air of the small apartment. For the thousandth time since crashing into Snowy Springs, gratitude filled her as she sat down to eat. The simple flavors of the food melted like a silent hymn of thankfulness.

Quickly eating and then cleaning up, Dakota headed for the bedroom and snuggled under the beautiful, colorful quilt on the bed. Aaron had assured her that it was okay for her to use it, and she so desperately wanted to believe that there were no strings attached and that the Bakker family had simply welcomed her in with no ulterior motives. But life rarely worked like that.

Sighing softly, she got comfortable. No doubt, tomorrow would bring more challenges of its own.

Chapter Seven

With a satisfied sigh, Dakota rested her weary body against the checkout counter of Snowy Springs Hardware. The first few days on any new job were always hard, but Aaron's definition of training consisted of giving her a tour of the store, a crash course in the inventory ledger, and leaving her alone for the rest of the day. A few trips next door in the mornings and the willing helpfulness of Sarah and Lana, Aaron's mother, had made the last few days far more bearable.

The store clock ticked over to four p.m. just as the jingle on the front door sounded. Aaron, along with a huge gust of snow, entered the store. He stamped his boots loudly on the welcome mat and shucked his coat.

"So, how did your day go?" he asked.

"Ah, well, thanks. Your mom and Sarah know a lot."

Aaron nodded, his expression sheepish. "I'm sorry I couldn't spend more time with you over the last few days, but the guys needed me to get on site. I'm sorry."

"It's all right. It's not an ordinary day if my heart doesn't feel like it's going to jump out of my chest each time the door chimes," she said, hoping to add some confidence to her voice. It still quivered a bit.

Aaron smiled in a way that showed he knew he was off the hook. "Thanks. I really do appreciate what you've been doing around here."

"So, how did the building go today?"

"Good. It would be better if I had more hands; but things are what they are, and I can only hope that it will be enough."

A new piece of Aaron's character slipped into place—not only was he kind and generous, but he was also someone who worked too hard.

"Do you have a minute? I just need to ask you something before you go."

"Sure."

"It won't take long." She could see the heavy weight of fatigue that hung on him.

Together, they walked to the delivery room at the back of the store. The room was filled with boxes of stock waiting to be unpacked. In the one corner was a small coffee table with a coffee machine and a small fridge.

"This delivery came today," she said, pointing to a large box of nuts, bolts, and screws. "I can't seem to find a purchase order. We looked for it, but . . . " She shrugged.

Aaron tiredly wiped his hand over his face and blew out a loud breath. "That's because I switched this order and charged it to the work site. These are for the community center project and not for the store."

"Okay, no problem. I'll call the supplier in the morning and sort it out."

"Really? You'd do that?"

"Yes, it is my job, isn't it?"

Her heart sped a little faster at the grateful smile she saw. "Are you okay?" The words tumbled from her mouth before she could caution herself against them.

Aaron paused, swallowed, and ran his hand through his messy hair. "Just got a lot on my mind." He sighed. He opened his mouth like he wanted to say something else but frowned, closing it again. Quiet filled the space between them. It wasn't an awkward silence more than a swelling tension.

Aaron lifted the ledger from the cash register and perused it. He smiled. "Thank you for taking care of the store," he said softly.

Heat flooded her cheeks, and she nodded. Aaron was breathtakingly handsome and as humble as a monk. She doubted he realized just how attractive he was; she was sure there must be a Mrs. Bakker waiting for him at home—another reason for her to keep her distance.

"Anyway, don't worry about it. I'm sure Mrs. Bakker is waiting for you at home, and this can wait until tomorrow." She turned to collect her bag behind the counter, ready for a hot cup of coffee and the soft sofa upstairs.

"No Mrs. Bakker," he said with grin. "And if that is your subtle way of asking if I'm single, the answer is yes."

Had someone turned up the heat in the store when she wasn't looking? "N-no, no. That wasn't why I said that," she quickly backtracked. Why *had* she said that? Although, she couldn't deny the shot of pleasure at his words.

Aaron raised his eyebrows playfully, all signs of his earlier distress gone. "Really? That's so interesting." He took a step closer to her.

Her pulse fluttered wildly. It was time for a hasty retreat. She crashed into the staircase and hurried up the steps, completely forgetting her bag behind the counter. She would come down later to get it. "Goodnight, Aaron," she called, halfway up the stairs.

A teasing laughter echoed in the empty store. Mortified, she ran the rest of the way and slammed the door behind her.

Ruffling through the mounds of clothes on her bed, she tucked them back into the duffel bag and waited. Her clothes still stank and needed a wash. Aaron would be in the store for a while still, and her bravery had long since left her. Silent as a mouse, she walked down the stairs, duffel bag over her shoulder. Aaron stood behind the checkout counter and paged slowly through the delivery ledger. A laptop and a cup of coffee rested beside him. His brow furrowed in concentration.

"It's no use trying to sneak past. The stairs creak," he said, his eyes trained on the ledger.

"I-I wasn't sneaking," she said and then straightened her spine. She didn't need to explain herself. "Can you point me in the direction of the laundromat, please?"

"Can't," he said.

"Why not?" Moving in and her work at the store had kept her busier than expected, and she desperately needed to find the laundromat becuase she was rapidly running out of clothes. The ones with Bobby's stench still lay tucked away under her bed. The idea of those anywhere near her made her skin crawl.

"They're already closed for the day. Look, Dakota, just come and use my washer; I promise I will leave you alone."

For a long moment, Dakota contemplated. Aaron had never done anything to hurt her, and as far as she could tell, he was a decent guy. "Okay, but just this once."

"Okay." Aaron closed the laptop and threw his coat over his shoulders. "Where's your coat?"

She shrugged. "I don't have one."

"Wait here a minute," he said and as quick as lightning was out the store and returned just as quickly with a beautiful, deep blue coat in hand. She raised her hands in protest. "Aaron, I . . . "

"Sarah says you can have this one." Aaron circled around her, slid the coat onto her shoulders, and gently squeezed them. "There, now, hopefully, you won't freeze to death."

"Thank you," she said. She was generating an account with Aaron that she had no hope of ever repaying, but she would try for as long as it took.

Aaron slung the duffel over his shoulder and held the door open to her. "My truck is just out front." He locked the door behind them. Seconds later, they pulled onto Main Street toward Aaron's house.

Aaron brought the truck to a stop outside a dark blue cottage. A large Christmas tree stood on the wide porch, which was adorned with a long row of flickering fairy lights dancing across the white awnings. The house looked surprisingly domesticated for a bachelor; but maybe Aaron had been married before, and his wife had left her mark on their house. She wasn't about to ask in case she made a fool of herself again.

"And here we are. It ain't much, but it's home," Aaron said with a grin. He leaned across the seat and reached for the bag behind her, crowding into her space.

She waited for the fear, but strangely, it didn't roar to life as it usually would have. No, instead, it seemed to rise like a slow hill and crashed down just as fast. The warmth of his body bled into hers, and she found herself taking a deep inhale of his unique scent.

Aaron stilled beside her as if aware of the riot moving through her body. He roughly cleared his throat. "Sorry," he muttered and dropped his arm, leaning back into his seat.

"It's okay," she said. "No harm done." Seeking a way to end the sparks buzzing between them, Dakota opened the truck door and hopped out. The cold night air slapped her warm cheeks and returned common sense to her brain. What business did she have finding a man like Aaron attractive? She'd just run away from one bad relationship, and now was not the time to consider starting a new one.

A few moments later, Aaron was by her side, duffel bag in hand. "You'll have to excuse the mess, but this morning was kind of crazy."

"I'm sure it can't be that bad."

"You haven't been into a bachelor's house, have you?"

Dakota paused and slowly shook her head. "No, but I do know what it's like to live with a man."

She couldn't say what response she'd expected from Aaron—maybe disgust to mark the kindness on his face or judgment to fill his eyes—but none of that came. He merely nodded, his face unreadable. "Not all men are the same."

She was beginning to see that although she'd known her whole life there were different kinds of men—ones like Bobby and ones like Aaron—in the last nine years, she'd forgotten the difference. *Or maybe you didn't want to see the difference.* Which was probably true. She had forgiven Bobby again and again, no matter what he'd done to her. She'd held onto the idea that he would change with time. He never had.

In two long strides, Aaron was at the door and had swung the door open. The warm light shining from the open door encouraged her into the house. She took another bracing breath and slowly stepped forward.

A small sound of surprise escaped her as she ran her eyes over the front room. It was almost magical. The tall Christmas tree she'd seen from outside was lit up with rows and rows of red and green Christmas lights. A bright fire blazed in the fireplace and gave the dark room a soft glow. All around the room, decorations hung.

"You must really love Christmas," she commented, handing the beautiful coat to him. Aaron stuck them both into a nearby closet and slid his hands into his back pockets.

His already wind-bitten cheeks turned ruddy. "Well, yes, I do it for my niece and nephew. Avery, my older sister, isn't really one for Christmas, so I kind of go overboard."

"You must be really close to them."

"Yeah, that's what family is about, isn't it? Looking out for each other and being there in the good and bad times."

It sounded so simple when he said it like that to her—if only she'd known what she was losing the day she'd left. "Not always." Not when daughters went out of their way to rebel against all that mattered to their parents. Why had she been so stubborn? Why hadn't she taken the help they offered?

"Dakota, are you all right?" Aaron asked. When had he come so close? The warmth of his hand resting on her shoulder sent a shock of awareness into her veins. Oh no, this couldn't be happening to her. She couldn't even think of it.

"Yes, yes, I'm fine," she said and deliberately moved away. The imprint burned into her skin and tingled, even though Aaron was a few good strides away from her.

Clutching her duffel protectively in front of her body, she cleared her parched throat. "Where is the washer?"

She could feel Aaron's curious eyes boring into her bent head. She wouldn't look up—not now. Not when the pain she tried so hard to ignore was probably written all over her face.

"Through the kitchen, on the left, and into the back. Detergent is on the top shelf," he said softly. She tried hard to ignore the obvious confusion in his tone. She was just as confused. She hadn't known a lot of nice men. In fact, the last nice man she had encountered was her brother, Kenny, and, of course, her dad.

"Thank you," she said. Not daring to raise her eyes, she scurried in the direction of his pointed hand.

Chapter Eight

What an enigma Dakota had turned out to be. One moment, she seemed calm, collected, and enjoyed his jokes. The next, she was the same wounded woman he'd met that first day at the hospital. Her aversion to his presence was fading, which was evident by her agreement to come with him tonight. But there was so much she was hiding from him.

The washer cycle turned over, and Dakota walked back into the living room, her hands worrying the hem of her sweatshirt.

"Coffee?" he asked.

"Oh, I don't want to trouble you."

"It's no trouble. Come sit in the kitchen. I'd like to get to know my new employee a bit more."

Dakota turned back into the room behind her and took a heavy seat at the counter.

Aaron joined her in the kitchen and busied himself with the coffee, setting two mugs beside her. "Cream and sugar?" he asked.

"Just black, thank you." She took a sip, a small smile blooming on that sweet mouth. "This is great coffee. Where did you get it?"

"From a friend in the next town. So, you know coffee. How is that?"

Dakota laughed. The sound was music to his ears and filled him with pleasure. "My mom and dad are coffee farmers. When I was young, we went to shows, where they would meet with other coffee growers and discuss farming techniques, the latest crop, and the state of the weather. I learned to appreciate the unique flavor of each brand and business."

"Where are your parents now? Do they still farm?"

"No, they sold the farm a few years back when . . . " She stuttered and took another hasty sip. "When Kenny died." Sadness burned in those stormy gray eyes again; her shoulders bowed under the weight of it.

Aaron gently took her hand from her cup and held it between his. Her skin was so soft under his wandering fingers as he waited for her to continue or compose herself. "Who's Kenny?"

"Kenny was my brother," she said. "He died when I was fifteen—a motor vehicle accident."

"I'm so sorry for your loss." What could he say? He knew all about loss; he'd thought he'd lost his best friend three years ago. Nothing compared to the loss of a loved one, whether parents or siblings. He continued gently massaging her hand between his, delighted that she hadn't pulled it away.

Minutes passed. "Three years ago, my best friend, Michael, went MIA in Afghanistan. We thought he was dead." The memories of the day they had received the news still clenched painfully in Aaron's chest.

Dakota's hands gripped his. "I'm sorry." She was; he could see it in her eyes. She could understand the devastation of death.

"Funny thing is, a few days ago, I got a call from Michael's brother, Noah, to say that he's alive." It was a joyous, mixed-up feeling.

"That's good, isn't it?" she asked.

"Yes, it's the best news I could have asked for."

"Then why do you look so worried?"

Should he tell her the reason—a reason that Sarah herself had not seen fit to tell him until Michael was long gone and she was falling apart?

"Sarah has been in love with Michael for years, and although I would like nothing more than my best friend back, I don't know what the news will do to her." He gently untwined their hands and leaned back into his seat. "When he went MIA, it almost killed her. I just don't want her to build up an expectation and see her get hurt."

Dakota nodded, anguish filling her eyes. "Would you rob your sister of the joy of knowing, even though she might get hurt? If given the choice, I would give anything to have Kenny back."

Aaron looked down at his hands. Would it be good for Sarah to know? Was he taking away the chance for her to be happy by not telling her?

"I guess I need to pray about it some more." He took her hand again, gently trailing his fingers over the length of her hand, noting the hard calluses formed. Why had he told her about Michael? She'd made it clear she didn't trust him. Why, then, did he desperately want her to see him as someone she could rely on?

At first, Dakota let him hold her hand before gently taking it away. "I think I need to check on the laundry," she said softly.

He instantly missed the warmth of her beside him as she rose and hurried from the room. He'd give her some time alone, if only to sort out his own roiling emotions. The feeling of protectiveness he had for Dakota was quickly becoming more. He wasn't sure what to do with that feeling any more than he was sure of what to do about Sarah. Instead of trying to figure it out, he busied himself with setting the dinner table. Emotions aside, they still had to eat.

Dakota stayed for a long time in the laundry room, and he let her have her space. The loud whirring of the dryer came from the room, and Dakota returned, her eyes and cheeks red. He wished he had the right to take her into his arms and hug her. She really looked like she needed someone to hold her.

"All right?" he asked and handed her a fresh cup of coffee.

"Yes, and thank you. It has been so long since I told anyone about Kenny. I guess the grief is still so near for me, even all these years later."

"What about your parents?" It had been the wrong question to ask, judging by the way Dakota's sorrowful expression closed.

Aaron turned to the fridge. "What would you like for dinner?" he asked, deliberately sticking his head into the fridge so she didn't see the acute disappointment he felt.

"Aaron, please don't," she said. Her hands trailed to the hem of her sweatshirt again. She was uncomfortable.

"Look, considering that load of washing you brought, you're going to be here a while. So, I have to eat; and you are here, so you can eat with me."

Dakota shook her head, her expression firmly in denial. "Aaron . . . "

Aaron gently took her hand again, and her words of protest faded away. He rather liked the idea of being attractive to her. "Just let me feed you. Please," he said and ran his fingers from the base of her wrist up to the soft yellow bruise in the crease of her arm. Expelling a ragged breath, Dakota nodded.

"Good. Now, what would you like? We have chicken parmesan, beef stew, or fish tacos."

"Which one is the easiest?"

"Probably the beef stew, seeing as Avery dropped some off while we were at work."

"Beef stew it is."

"Are you sure?" he asked. He sensed, for some reason, that Dakota would give him an answer that wouldn't have anything to do with her real choice. Her choice would be the one that was the least inconvenient for him.

"Yes." And off she went to the laundry room again.

The large portion of beef stew landed with a wet plop into the pot. Avery always said to warm it slowly, or else it would burn. He was a relatively good cook and could appreciate the soundness of her advice. Pretty soon, the kitchen was filled with the smell of cooking stew. He rinsed off the rice and placed it in the pot for the last few minutes of cooking. The dryer came on again, and the washer whirred in tandem.

"Dinner will be ready in ten," he said.

"Oh, good. I'm starving."

Aaron's mouth went dry at the sight of Dakota—washing basket on her hip, her blonde hair in a messy ponytail, and her eyes soft, shoulders relaxed. Man, what he would give to come home each day to her like this. The thought stunned him. This was a woman he'd known for little more than a week and who clearly had more secrets than the United States government. But there was something right about her here, with him in his house.

Ruffling his hand through his hair, he turned his attention back to the dinner preparations, mechanically filling the plates and setting them back on the table for dinner.

"Dinner's up," he said just as Dakota had finished folding the huge pile she'd taken from the dryer. She looked pleased with something—and her small smile made him want to ask—but would she clam up again? There was only one way to find out.

"You look pleased with yourself," he said cautiously.

Dakota beamed. "That was the last load. All my clothes smell fresh and clean, not like smoke and booze." Her eyes went wide before she dropped them to her hands again.

There was something in the way she said the words that made him want to dig deeper, but at the sight of her slightly pink cheeks and the discomfort coming off her in waves, he left it alone. "Glad I could help."

Dakota took the place set beside him at the table and toyed with the glass Santa figurines that served as his salt and pepper shakers. "Cute."

"I thought so. I got them as a gag gift from Sarah last Christmas," he said. As if it was the most natural thing in the world, he took her hand in his and bowed his head. "Thank You, Father, for Your abundant provisions. Please bless this meal for us. Amen."

The distant clang of the dryer was the only sound to be heard as they dug into their food.

A groan of pleasure caught his attention. Dakota's eyes were closed, her expression one of pure bliss as she ate beside him. "This is delicious, Aaron. Do I have Avery to thank or you?"

"Avery made the base. I added something to it to make it mine."

"Wow, this is probably the best beef stew I've ever had in my life." Her utter honestly meant it was likely to be true.

"Stop, stop. You're making me blush."

Dakota chuckled. "Oh look, Mr. Manly Man blushes," she said. Her finger lightly tapped the stubble on his cheek.

Aaron froze, his gaze locked with hers, his heart thundering in response. A long moment passed. Those pink lips begged him closer. As bizarre as it sounded, he wanted to see if they were as soft as they looked.

Eyes wide with shock, Dakota withdrew her hand and took another bite of her food. "You should sell this stuff. I would be your first customer."

"Glad you're enjoying it. You can come for dinner anytime," he said and hoped Dakota would take him up on the offer. It was nice to have her here, with him.

Dakota's hand paused for a moment and scraped the remains of her food together. "Thank you," she said.

She was in full retreat again. He could tell by the slight shake in her eating hand and the busyness of the other. Sighing softly, he finished his food and then stood and placed his plate in the sink. The dryer hummed one last time, and then it was silent.

"That's the last one," she said as if to herself.

The night was ending too soon, and Aaron was at a loss as to how to make it continue. Dakota stood and ditched her plate in the sink and then hurried off to the laundry room while he packed away the remains of dinner.

An idea formed. Sarah had said she'd dropped off a batch of his mother's cookies. It would be a shame for Dakota to leave without trying one.

A loud bustle came from the laundry room, and Dakota came out again, basket full. She settled into the sofa and began to fold her laundry. As if sensing him, she stopped, a slight tremor in her hands. "Sorry to take over like this. It's just that they'll crease if I don't fold them right away."

"Take your time. I don't mind. In fact, I was wondering if you'd like another cup of coffee. My mom made cookies, and it would really be a shame if they went to waste because I couldn't eat them all."

The tremors faded, and a small smile ticked up. "As if that was even a remote possibility. A strapping man like you unable to finish a jar of cookies? Unlikely."

"You think I'm strapping, is it?"

Color filled her cheeks again, and she turned her focus back to the laundry. "It was about the cookies."

"Right. How about that coffee?"

"I'm sure I've imposed enough on your time, Aaron. You really should just take me home, please."

It was time to put a misconception to rest. Aaron gently took the clothes from Dakota's hands and pulled her to her feet. He moved closer, so she couldn't possibly misunderstand what he would say next. Being this close to her sent his heart on a rampage, but it wasn't about attraction now—even though there was plenty of it.

"Dakota, I want you to hear what I'm about to say, okay?" He waited for her to nod. "You are not a bother to me, not now and not ever. You can be honest with me. I don't mind."

The pale gray of her eyes intensified, and a shuddering breath blew against his neck. He wanted to kiss her—oh, so much—but that wasn't what she needed. Fighting back the urge, he let go of her hands and went back to the kitchen. He returned a few minutes later with fresh coffee and a plate of double chocolate cookies. Dakota sat beside a neat pile of clean clothes, her eyes clearer than he'd yet seen them.

"Black coffee and the finest double chocolate cookies in town," he said and placed both mugs, along with the plate, on the coffee table nearby.

"Thank you."

He was relieved to see she didn't move away when his hand brushed hers. He sat down beside her on the sofa and took a sip of his coffee. Dakota did the same, moving until she was comfortable on the sofa. It warmed him to see her guard down, even if it was only for this moment.

"Would now be a good time to ask how you came to be in Snowy Springs?" he asked. The soft cushions of his sofa gave way under his weight as he leaned back into it. The air around them tensed.

Dakota sighed. "I made some bad decisions and needed to get away from them. Anyway, I'm here now."

There was much more to the story than she was telling him; he knew that maybe with time and persistence, she would let him in. Quelling the urge to touch her again, he took another sip of his coffee. Unable to leave the matter in the air, he said, "Dakota, I hope with time and familiarity, you'll trust me with your secrets one day."

Denial immediately hitched her face, and her hands became busy. Aaron swallowed back his disappointment. Time—it was always about time.

"Are you ready to go?" he asked when the coffee was gone and one cookie remained on the plate.

"Thank you again for your help. I don't know what I would've done."

"No problem. Let's get you home."

Together, they stood. Aaron gathered Dakota's duffel, careful to not disturb the clothes inside, and hiked it onto his shoulder.

Chapter Nine

There was something unbelievably attractive about a man who could work with his hands. Dakota took a minute to appreciate the sight of Aaron bent over the wood saw, a large plank moving deftly through his hands. Attraction bounced in her chest as he paused to wipe the sweat from his forehead with the rag beside him and settled his goggles back over his handsome face.

Get back to work, girl; he doesn't see you that way. There had been a few moments last night when she'd doubted the wisdom of those words, but Aaron had come into the shop bright and early and acted as if nothing was different between them. But it was.

The saw continued to hum. She needed to get back to work. The orders wouldn't process themselves.

The door opened with a loud rattle, and Sarah entered the store. "Hi, Sarah, he's in the workroom."

"I do need to speak with Aaron, but I actually came to see you. Mom and I were wondering if you'd like to join us for dinner tonight."

"Will Aaron be there?"

A mischievous smile tipped Sarah's lips. "Only if you want him to be. If it's too awkward having your boss there, I can tell him to go away."

A loud clearing of a throat broke Sarah into giggles. "I heard that," Aaron said and shook a cloud of dust in Sarah and Dakota's direction.

"Gross, Aaron. I have a meeting with a supplier this afternoon. I don't want to be covered in sawdust."

"Sorry," he said, his smile completely unapologetic. "What's this I hear about dinner?"

"You're not invited." Sarah grinned at Dakota. She smiled back. Sarah was becoming like the sister she'd never had.

"Wasn't that Dakota's decision?" he asked. He turned those brown eyes on her, and her knees turned to liquid.

"I, uh . . . Uh, really, it's okay," she said. "I don't mind."

Aaron frowned, and Sarah glanced between them. "Okay, if you're sure. At six, okay? Aaron can bring you."

"Wait, Sarah . . . " But the door was already closing behind her. Aaron grinned and—oh goodness, even sweat looked attractive on the man.

"I don't have to come if you want a night just with girls or something." His care softened something in her heart, although a whisper of fear slid up her spine. Being vulnerable meant she could get hurt, and she'd been hurt enough for a lifetime.

"It's your family, Aaron. I don't want to come between you. Besides, Sarah did invite both of us."

He stared at her and then nodded. "Okay. If you're sure. I'll come by at 5:30 to get you. Wear something comfortable. If I know my mom, there's bound to be too much food." With a gentle smile, Aaron sauntered off back to the work room.

It had been the strangest day having him in the shop. When she'd come down the stairs that morning, he'd told her something about a work delay and then had disappeared into the work room. She was really beginning to wonder if there was more to it than that. For whatever reason, he chose to stay. She was glad for the company. The store did get quiet at times.

Work went quickly. Mabel from the hospital called to check on her, and Mr. Bouwer came for another axe and saw. Apparently, his were too blunt to be of much use this winter. Before she could blink for too long, four p.m. toned on the store clock.

"You go get ready. I'll close up and see you in an hour," Aaron said as he grabbed his coat and pulled a dark green hat over his unruly hair. Was it as soft as it looked? The style begged her hands to run through the long lengths, and she clamped her hands together behind the counter, lest Aaron see their movement. This was bad.

"Sure," she said breathlessly.

Aaron quirked an eyebrow. "It's just a dinner. I promise they aren't that scary."

Bless him, he thought her nerves had to do with the dinner. She was nervous about being in Lana's home, but that nervousness was minuscule in comparison to the driving force of unrest he caused simply by standing too close to her. She forced herself not to move. If she did, it would give him an indication of what she was feeling.

"I know," she said just as breathlessly as before.

Aaron moved closer to her, and she crashed into the counter behind her. The fire burning in his eyes ignited one of her own. It was wonderful and frightening in equal measure.

Side-stepping Aaron, she hurried away from the temptation of him. "I'll be ready by five," she said, taking the first step.

Aaron watched her with a burning intensity and slowly nodded. "I'll be here."

The steps disappeared under the clatter of her shoes as she ran up, her heart beating a mile a minute on the way. She was in trouble.

She took the longest shower she'd ever taken in an effort to calm her pounding heartbeat. As soon as it was under control, she'd think about Aaron and have to start the activity all over again. How was she going to manage tonight? She could scarcely be in the same room as the man without wanting him to drop the genteelness and kiss the sense out of her.

The idea of kissing Aaron was both thrilling and terrifying. The first time Bobby had kissed her had been nice, but he'd never made her pulse rush off by being in the same room as she. Maybe that was what made him so mad.

The cheery adrenaline pulsating inside her came to a grinding halt. She had to stop these silly thoughts of her and Aaron. They were something that could never happen. He was a good, gentle man; and she was a broken, cowardly hypocrite. Panic quaked in her knotted stomach as she imagined the look in Aaron's eyes when he found out what she truly was—what lengths she'd gone to in order to keep Bobby happy, what price she'd paid for her compliance.

Ignoring the bright floral dress she'd chosen earlier, hoping to catch Aaron's eye, she slipped on a pair of black dress pants and a loose, deep blue blouse. It was more business and less flirty. With any luck, Aaron would see it as such and leave her alone.

When the store bell jingled an hour later, Dakota had her game face on, her foolishness firmly locked behind the same walls she kept her heart behind.

"You look nice," Aaron said as he came to a stop in front of her.

And he looked wonderful. Black jeans emphasized his long legs; a deep green button-up snugly covered his broad shoulders; and whatever aftershave he was wearing was designed for temptation. Dakota firmly took her racing pulse in hand. No, she would get through this dinner and then make an effort to put some much-needed distance between her and Aaron before it was too late. Or maybe it already was.

When Aaron reached for her hand, she evaded him. A deep frown crossed his brow, almost faltering her resolve. It was the right thing to do for the both of them.

"Are you ready to go?" he asked. His eyes were unfathomable.

"Almost. Let me just get my purse." And her sanity. Dakota quickly grabbed her purse and hurried back to Aaron, who waited patiently with her coat. He held it up, and she slipped her arms into it. Her breath seized as Aaron came around and zipped it up. He gently tapped her nose when he was done.

"There. Now, we're ready," he said, tenderness melting the firm grip she had on her restraint. He took her hand, and butterflies tripped over themselves to dance with feeling. She didn't pull away again. Her resolve stank.

Aaron locked the store behind them and then opened the truck door for her; she climbed in and took a deep breath. Like the heavenly smell on Aaron, the truck smelled just as good. *Please let me make it through this evening without making a mistake.* Mistakes came with a cost, and the cost of softening her heart to Aaron was too high.

"You're awfully quiet," he said after climbing in the truck. Her hand rested with his on his thigh as he began to drive. She didn't have the heart to take it away.

"Just thinking." How was she going to get herself out of this? How, when the time came, was she going to leave Aaron and Snowy Springs behind?

"Something serious?" he asked.

"How do you do that?"

"Do what?"

"Seem to be reading my mind."

"It's a gift. But seriously, what's going on in that beautiful head of yours?"

Her chest swelled with the word "beautiful." He thought she was beautiful. Something she hadn't known for years. "I was wondering about Sarah, actually. She seems like a lovely person. How come she's not married?"

Aaron frowned. Did he know she'd been thinking about them and the sheer impossibility of the situation? "Remember, I told you about Michael last night?"

Dakota nodded. Of course. Sarah was in love with Aaron's best friend, Michael.

"Doesn't he see her that way?" After all, that situation didn't sound too dire.

"No." A deep pain darkened Aaron's face. "Even though they've found him, I'm not sure he could return the feelings she's held for him so long."

"I'm sorry, Aaron. He sounds like quite a guy."

"Yeah, he is . . . er, was. I don't know."

Overcome with emotion, she held his hand tighter; he squeezed her hand back. What was it about this man that hurt so deeply and yet could be so kind and gentle?

"I missed him, you know? He was my best friend and like a brother to me. The things we got up to as kids . . . If I think about them now, I about have a stroke. In every memory, he's there."

Dakota swallowed hard. "I feel like that about my parents."

Aaron brought the car to a stop outside a beautiful colonial. The truck went quiet as he turned the key, but he didn't climb out. He waited.

Dakota took a deep breath. "I haven't seen my parents in five years. When I left their house, I was an angry teenager. Kenny had been dead two years. The pain and grief of losing him was gradually destroying my family. My parents fought all the time and cried the rest. They seemed to forget that I was there, suffering just like them. The day I graduated, I moved out. I haven't been home since. Five years ago, I cut all ties."

Strong, comforting arms pulled her into a hard chest, and the smell of him invaded her senses. She buried her face into the folds of his shirt and let the tears she'd been set on hiding come. For a long while, he held her, being a pillar on which she could lean.

Eventually, she pushed back, hiccupping. "I'm sorry. I've ruined your shirt," she said feebly, wiping at the wet patch at the center of his chest, surprised to see his cheeks wet, too.

"It'll dry." He handed her a tissue from his pocket and quietly wiped the wetness there. Time seemed to stand still until a hard knock on the window ripped it away.

"Are you coming in? Mom's about dying in there."

Aaron chuckled softly under his breath, and Dakota grinned, thankful for the interruption.

"I think we better get inside."

Dakota nodded and allowed him to draw her out of the truck and into the house.

"Aaron, may I speak with you?" Sarah asked as she shut the front door behind them. Aaron drew the coat from Dakota's shoulders and smiled as his mother immediately took her by the hand and led her into the kitchen. "Sure."

Sarah waited until he had taken off his own coat and put it away before gesturing for him to follow her down the short hallway to his father's study. The study still smelled like his father's cedar aftershave, even after four years. A set of dusky, brown leather single sofas were arranged in a circle in front of his father's old oak desk. Memories sprang from the many pictures along the wooden walls. Bookshelves lined the walls to his left and in front of him. His father had always been an avid reader; perhaps that was why his mother had opened the bookshop—in honor of his memory.

"What's up?"

Sarah thrust her curled fists into her hips and glared at him. Her lips wobbled as her eyes filled with tears.

Aaron crossed the room to her. "What is it?"

"Why didn't you tell me?" she asked. Accusation bled from her eyes, along with an emotion so pained, it made his chest ache. "Why didn't you tell me about Michael?" Unushered tears joined the pain crushing him.

His stomach hardened with guilt. "I'm sorry, Sarah, I didn't know how to tell you." Emotions flickered in quick succession over her face until she nodded. "I don't know if we will even get to see him. He's in Denver with his family, and we're here."

"Even then, you should have told me. Aaron, I saw him. In Denver. I saw Michael and the others. He looks . . . " Her expression crumpled into tears, and he pulled her close.

"I'm sorry, Sarah. I didn't mean to hurt you," he said, hoping it was enough to explain why he hadn't found the courage to tell his sister about what was going on. "I think I am still coming to terms with the fact that he's alive. After all this time." Tears slowly trailed down Sarah's cheeks.

"He looks so broken. Aaron, the pain in his eyes . . . " She cried harder.

It seemed like it was his night to be cried on. First Dakota and now Sarah. He was turning into a sap. When Sarah eventually stilled, he handed her his remaining tissues. "Are you going to be okay?"

Sarah nodded, although he could still see her heartbreak in her eyes. "I think so. What can we do?"

"We need to pray for him—and for Dakota."

Sarah's sad expression lit with amusement. "We will. I like her, and I know Mom does, too."

"Yeah, me, too," he admitted, if only to himself and his sister. He cared about Dakota.

"Do you think she'll stay?" Sarah asked, curling her arm into his and turning him toward the door. "I don't want you to get hurt again."

That was an excellent question. He hoped Dakota would settle in Snowy Springs. However, he wasn't sure she would. "I guess, only time will tell."

Chapter Ten

The shop door closed with a slight rattle behind Aaron. Dinner with Aaron's family had been a wonderful mix of laughter and veiled remarks. More than once, she'd found herself blushing at the direction of Lana's questions. Lana had made it no secret that she wanted her son to find a good woman for a wife. Dakota flushed when Lana's hopeful gaze flashed in Dakota's direction. Lana didn't know Dakota's past, didn't know her. If she did, she would never think Dakota was good enough for her son. Still, it hurt, the thought of him with someone else.

"I'll see you in the morning?" Aaron asked. His black jacket sat snuggly across his broad shoulders, outlining the lean muscles of his upper body. Butterflies fluttered inside her stomach.

"Ah, yes," she said hoping her attraction to him wasn't written all over her face. Aaron reached out to her, gently folding her hand in his. It took her a moment to realize that she hadn't flinched at the movement. In fact, a whole different set of tingles raced up her arm. She shivered.

"Are you cold?"

"N-no." She cleared the dryness from her throat, "No, I'm fine." But Aaron had already enclosed her with his arms. Dakota laid her head on his chest, slowly raising her arms to encircle his waist.

Aaron drew a deep breath, the rapid staccato of his heart beat in her ear.

"I had a great time tonight with you. And I think I need to apologize for the direction of my mother's questions. She worries. Ever since . . . " He swallowed hard and released her from his embrace. "That doesn't matter now. Anyway, sleep tight, Dakota." His tone was regretful, like he loathed to end their night together.

For a long moment, they faced each other. The air filled with something, like a force of emotions swirling around them. It was as if he was trying to communicate the words he hadn't said out loud, a silent message that she struggled to interpret.

"It's okay. It's just—"

"You miss your family?"

Dakota gasped, stunned by his intuition, by the way he saw right through her. No one had done that since Kenny. He'd been her hero, her best friend, and the person she went to when life was hard. But then, he had died, and she'd been left on her own.

"More than I could possibly know. It's strange. It's been so long since I've thought of them, but now, I just want to pick up the phone and tell them how sorry I am for everything."

"Why don't you?" Aaron slipped his hand into his jacket pockets forcefully, like he was fighting the urge to draw her near again. She wished he would. Maybe then she wouldn't feel like a satellite floating endlessly through space.

She forced a chuckle. "Well, there is the slight issue of a phone. I don't have one."

Without making a fuss, Aaron pulled a white, square box out of his pocket. "That reminds me. I got this for you today. I forgot to give it to you." He was stretching the truth a little, she could tell. He wanted to help without looking like he was helping. This man was determined to undermine everything she thought she knew. This endeared him to her all the more. Aaron was a good man. Good, kind, and selfless. All the things she was not.

"Aaron . . . " she began.

"Look, I know what you're going to say—I shouldn't have, how could you pay me back, and so on, but . . . "

Dakota tenderly cupped his cheek, effectively rendering him mute. "Thank you," she whispered leaning up to kiss his smooth cheek. Before he could react, she took the phone from his hand and hurried up the stairs to the apartment.

"Good night, Aaron," she said as she reached the top of the stairs. An almost silent chuckle reached her ears. Insufferable man.

The mobile phone shook in her hand as she debated. It had been so long since she'd called her parents. What if their number had changed? And worse still, what if they didn't even want to speak to her? What if they ignored her like they had all those years ago? What if they saw the call and somehow knew it was her and didn't answer?

On and on, the questions circled. They shriveled up her courage and dumped it into the black hole she carried in her heart. A growl of frustration passed her lips. This endless debating was getting her nowhere. The phoned loudly clattered onto the bedside cabinet as she sat heavily on the beautiful quilt. Her hands smoothed over the cotton knots that formed a large cloud on the quilt. What time must have been spent on each stitch and picture to make something so beautiful.

The phone pinged loudly in the emptiness. She startled, laughing at herself. It was just her here; there was no need to be afraid. The message app opened with a swipe of her hand. One message from Aaron.

Do you want to go to church with us tomorrow?

She toyed with the phone, tossing it again and again onto the bed cover. Could God help her to repair the relationship with her parents despite all Dakota had done to break it?

Her relationship with church had been dismal growing up. It was gone by the time Kenny had died and she'd made the decision that would change her life. Yet there was still a piece of her that ached to belong somewhere, longed to be loved despite what she'd done. Perhaps she would take Aaron up on his invitation and go to church. After all, everything else she'd tried had only made her life worse.

While she prepared for bed, she typed a quick yes and sent the message.

"Are we in the right place?" she asked Aaron as they came to stop outside a large white building. The church's pale steeple stood tall in the skyline. Wide open stretches of farmland surrounded the majestic, old building. People milled around the half-open, white doors smiling and laughing. It was a joyous sound, like something mysteriously happy was about to happen.

"Yes, why? Welcome to Snowy Springs Community Church."

Church? Where were the somber faces and stiff suits? Where were the judgmental glances and the feeling of misery she'd so often encountered in a building like this? Someone beside her laughed, and she quickly turned to study the woman. The woman was young, probably near the same age as her. Her long, blonde hair shone in the light, and her smile was just as infectious. Her gaze swept to the side, her eyes widening. It took Dakota a moment to see that the thing the woman was staring at was Aaron, who stood as stiff as a post beside her.

"Are you ready to go in?" he asked kindly, although his gaze kept glancing at the woman. Was she someone he knew? Ignoring the unease that tensed her shoulders, she allowed Aaron to draw her into the large, open hall.

"You look lovely, by the way," he whispered as a man with a wide smile and dressed in jeans and a button-up showed them to a seat. The hall was pretty full, though it was the beautiful music that held her attention. It was like the sound of angels singing some beautiful harmony that dug deep into her bone-dry heart. Her heart moved with a painful thud.

She looked up to see Aaron was still waiting for a response from her. Oh, what was it again? "Thank you," she said and took the seat beside Sarah, who gave her a warm welcome.

"Dakota, it's so wonderful to see you today. How did you sleep?"

"Okay, I guess." Truth was that most of the night had been spent staring at the phone, mooning over Aaron, and sipping a strong cup of cocoa.

Aaron had asked the same question. She had answered as truthfully and uninformatively as possible and then ignored his frown. She'd tried her best to erase the dark rings with makeup. She must've not been very successful. What did he have to frown about when he was watching some gorgeous woman who would make a much better match for him than she?

What was she thinking? There was no "them," and therefore, she had nothing to be jealous of. Jealously was something a person felt when they loved someone, and she sure didn't love Aaron. She merely liked him—as a friend—a kind and gorgeous friend.

Sarah's encouraging smile bent into a deep frown, and Dakota cringed back. As she dropped her gaze, she saw Sarah's expression remain in one of disgruntlement. Peeking under her lashes, Dakota followed to where Sarah was looking, and sure enough, it was on the blonde woman—the one Aaron had watched so carefully outside. Why were they both looking at the woman with such dislike? Sarah and Aaron were wonderful people. What had the blonde woman done?

Curiosity got the better of her. While Aaron was distracted speaking to an elderly man, Dakota tugged at Sarah's hand to get her attention.

"Sarah, who is that woman?" she asked.

"Oh, that's just Lacey," Sarah said. Even in just the short time she had known her, Dakota knew Sarah wouldn't hurt a fly, but the level of disgust with which she said "Lacey" confirmed Dakota's suspicions. What had this Lacey woman done to two of her favorite people?

The music started up again, and Dakota pushed the mystery of Lacey from her mind. For the next thirty minutes, she listened as the words of the songs washed over her and gently massaged the ache in her heart. She didn't know any of the songs, although the words seemed to be designed just for her.

At last, a man stood and walked up to a brown, wooden table. It was a tall one, like the ones a person would see in a bar. He laid down a large, black book. Dakota shivered. She remembered that book. From that book, judgment would come. She stiffened. As if sensing her unease, Aaron reached out for her hand, giving her plenty of time to pull away before grasping it firmly in his. His warmth helped calm her anxiety.

The man began to speak, his words holding Dakota captive. "Matthew 11:28 says, *'Come to me, all you who are weary and burdened, and I will give you rest.'*"

Rest—what a wonderful idea. To stop running. To stop jumping at every shadow. To stop being so afraid. A burden—oh, what a burden she had carried all this time—the secret that was destroying her, the secret that only Bobby knew. And if Aaron knew, he would beat her just like Bobby had. But the idea of rest . . .

She listened closer, drinking up each word like water—like she was parched, and the words were the freshest hydration to her.

"All of us carry a burden. Burdens come in different shapes and sizes. Maybe it's the burden of losing a loved one and never moving past the grief. Maybe it's the burden of a relationship gone wrong, and you feel there is nothing you can do to fix it. Or maybe it's the burden of a mistake you made that aches deep in your heart, day and night.

"As people on this earth, we face burdens, and we have challenges. In these cases, we look for ways to validate our burdens by hanging onto our bitterness; after all, the fault rests with that person, thing, or circumstance. How could it possibly be your fault or responsibility to fix it?

"But this is not the way God looks at our burdens. He looks at them through the eyes of His overwhelming love for us and His mercy by the grace given from the sacrifice Jesus made. In Psalm 86:5, David says, 'You, Lord, are forgiving and good, abounding in love, to all who call to you.'"

The pastor continued, "God's love and mercy can overcome any burdens we have and any challenge we face if we would just let Him, if we would invite Him into our lives and allow Him to take our burdens away. But this can be done only through the healing power of forgiveness. God will and can forgive us.

"But what about you, friend? Are you willing to forgive—not only yourself but the person who has hurt you? Only then can you find true peace. Forgiveness is as much for the giver as for the receiver."

Dakota so wanted to believe that it was possible that God loved her enough to forgive her for the horrendous thing she'd done. A wave of emotion clogged her throat, forcing a gasp from her chest. Pain like she'd never experienced pressed against the protection of her heart. It begged her to let it go, to call on this loving God she remembered as a child—to give Him the heavy burden of guilt, bitterness, and shame she carried.

Lord, help me. I don't know how to trust. Show me how to trust You and Your love. I want to be Your child.

The rest of the service passed in a blur, her mind lost in the push and pull of emotions. When Aaron took her hand once more, she knew the service was over. She shouldn't let him hold her hand, but she was powerless to let go—not when she so desperately needed someone to hang on to. Warmth filled her chest, and had her heart not been so heavy, she might have smiled. Something new, warm, and comforting was slowly overcoming her fear, filling her with joy.

The terror she'd experienced at first in his presence was gone. She knew without asking why. Aaron was a gentleman. He showed her day by day that real men didn't treat women like pieces of used pottery to be discarded or burned up and reused—or as their own personal punching bag. No, Aaron had shown her respect and kindness, made her feel like she mattered—just like her daddy.

She wiped at her eyes—maybe her makeup had escaped unscathed—and walked out into the cold, gleaming sunshine. The lightness in her chest told her she had taken a step toward hope.

Chapter Eleven

"Aaron? Do you have a minute?" Lacey asked, ignoring the fact that Aaron had his arm firmly wrapped around Dakota's waist. His grip tightened, as Dakota stiffened beside him, wariness crossing her lovely features as her gaze bounced from him to Lacey.

"Dakota, why don't you come with me?" Sarah asked.

Aaron dropped his arm from Dakota's waist, allowing her to be led away by Sarah and his mother. He watched them leave before turning around. Lacey's wide, blue eyes stared up at him, pleading for understanding.

"What is it, Lacey?" he asked with far more patience than he felt.

Lacey's open expression crumbled; the mouth he'd kissed so often and had hoped to kiss for the rest of his life fell into a pout. "I'm sorry. I shouldn't be here," she said softly. She turned to leave, shoulders slumped.

Compassion filled him. "No, I'm sorry. I'm being incredibly rude. I'm sure you understand."

Lacey inclined her head, her expression sad. "Daddy hasn't been well the last few weeks, and I came into town to see him. I won't be here much longer, but I wanted to tell you how sorry I am for leaving you the way I did. I don't think an explanation would make any difference, but I had to say it."

She did this now? After months and months of wondering and mourning the life that would never be his, now Lacey came back to town to say she was sorry?

"Why?"

"Why did I leave?"

"No, why did you apologize?"

Lacey's angel face gave a wobbly smile. "Aaron, you were the boy I loved when I was in high school. When we came back from college, I began to doubt. I should have said something sooner. I don't know why I didn't. As the wedding got closer and closer, I knew I had to do something, so I ran to Dallas. Like a coward, I ran instead of facing you and the truth. I'm sorry."

Here was the closure he needed. Although he had healed from her desertion, it was good to understand why Lacey had left. It was not something he had done but rather something that had changed between them. If he looked past his anger at Lacey, he knew they were not the same people who had fallen in love in high school. Lacey had done them a favor by leaving instead of going through with the wedding. The relief of it all made him smile.

"There's nothing to forgive." Aaron opened his arms wide, and Lacey stepped into them. He hugged her, silently saying goodbye to their shared history. "Take care of yourself, Lacey. And have a happy life."

Lacey wiped at her eyes. "You, too, Aaron. And by the looks of it, you've found someone already."

"Dakota? No, we're only friends."

Lacey laughed. "Aaron, I've known you for most of my life; and from what I've seen, it's far more than that." She waved and rejoined her parents at their truck.

What did Lacey mean—"there was more to it than that"? Was there? Was Dakota beginning to soften toward him? She allowed him to hold her hand and hug her in times of distress, or was there more to it? Shaking his head, he ruffled his hair as he headed for his truck. He must be insane for thinking it, but it did make sense. She didn't seem to mind when he'd wrapped his arm around her waist earlier, and she did make his blood flow faster. And what of the night before? He was sure the attraction arching between them was not one-sided.

It would be better if he left it at friends and stopped anything else from happening between them. Dakota would leave town when her car was ready, and he would go on with his life. A shaft of pain struck his chest as he thought of that inevitable day. His emotions were tangled up with Dakota already, and if he was a wise man, he would keep his distance from her. Heartbreak was a painful lesson to learn, and he did not want to take that class again.

Dakota and Sarah's voices evaporated as he approached. With troubled expressions, they stared at him. Dakota's gaze swung to Lacey and then back to him. Her expression cleared of all emotion, a hollow emptiness filling her eyes.

"Everything okay?" he asked Dakota, who dropped her gaze to the hem of her jacket and slid it between her fingers. She did not look up at him.

"I don't feel very well. Sarah, would you mind taking me home?" she asked.

"Sure. I'll see you later at Mom's," Sarah said to Aaron. "My car is over there."

Dakota turned and marched toward the car. Her body language screamed rejection. Sarah squeezed his hand and hurried after her. Soon, they were on their way. Aaron stood for a moment. Should he follow? Everything in him wanted to, if just to find out what was going on with Dakota.

He opened the door of his truck.

"How are the repairs for the community center coming?" Will Evans asked, coming alongside him. Will was on the Christmas Committee and a pain in Aaron's side.

Aaron grimaced. He didn't have time for this; he needed to get to Dakota and see what had upset her so much. Sighing, he ran his hand over his face. "We are working as fast as we can. Lord willing, we'll be done on time."

"I don't know, Aaron. The damage seems too extensive. Are you sure we shouldn't subcontract it out? I have a cousin in Denver who I am sure could lend us a hand."

Rapidly running out of patience, Aaron waved his hand to stop Will. "Thank you, Will. We'll have it done. Townsfolk take care of town matters." Ignoring whatever next helpful bit of advice he was sure Will had to offer, Aaron climbed into the cab and slammed the door.

Rushing to leave, he spun in a cloud of dust out of the church parking lot. He'd have to send another contribution for new gravel in the lot again sometime. Minutes later, he was outside the shop. Sarah's SUV was parked beside the curb. The ladies were obviously still inside. Aaron swung open the door and hurried up the stairs.

Sarah and Dakota sat huddled on one sofa in the living room, coffee mugs before them. They both paused as he entered.

"Why did you leave so quickly?" he asked.

Dakota took a long swallow of the coffee.

"I'll wait downstairs," Sarah said by way of excusing herself.

Aaron boldly took the coffee mug from Dakota's hands. His action surprised him, nullifying his earlier advice to himself. Dakota looked stunned. Her cold hands instantly warmed in his, and he felt his heart thump hard behind his rib cage.

"I suppose you've come to kick me out?" she asked. Her expression was sad yet accepting like she'd been expecting this turn of events.

"Kick you out? Why would I kick you out?" What was going on here?

"So, she can move back in?"

Her voice was barely above a whisper. What madness was this woman thinking?

"Dakota, Lacey isn't coming back. She's leaving in a few days to go back to Dallas."

Palpable relief bloomed on Dakota's face; and Aaron, try as he might, couldn't suppress his wide smile or the warmth her jealousy brought.

"I thought . . . " She flushed, pressing her lips together.

"Dakota, the place is yours as long as you want it." *Please don't go.* The thought settled inside him, expanding until it filled every nook and cranny of his heart. "But what I want to know is why you were so upset about Lacey coming back." He needed to know. Did she feel the same crazy attraction he felt?

"Oh, well, I, ah . . . didn't want to have to look for a new place. You know what a bother that can be." She let out a weak laugh. He knew she was lying through her teeth. The feeling inside him expanded.

"Were you jealous?" he teased.

Bright color spread like a river over Dakota's fine-boned features. "No, why would I be?" She shifted, threading the hem of her sweater in and out between her fingers. She *was* jealous of the thought of him and Lacey. What did that mean?

"You were." Had Lacey been right? Could he push his luck a little further? "Dakota . . . " He carefully wrapped his arms around her body. When there was no resistance, he pulled her fully against him and held her tight. Her soft hair brushed his cheek, and a shiver passed through him.

Dakota sat with rigid resistance and then, muscle by muscle, relaxed against him, acquiescing to his touch. The riot in his chest might kill him, but there was no way he was letting go. She burrowed closer, pressing her face into his chest. His pulse sped up again, and the urge to kiss her almost overwhelmed him. It would not be a good idea to give into the urge, not when she was finally softening. He wished he could hold onto the moment forever.

Aaron ended the embrace and sat back, giving Dakota the space she needed. Something momentous had happened to Dakota during the church service and possibly between them. She needed time to process, as did he.

"Would you like to come for lunch? I know Mom won't mind, and Sarah's about ready to kill me." He waited, hopeful until Dakota slowly nodded.

"Okay."

Care for her nearly overwhelmed him. "And maybe later, I could take you around town to see the sights." After such a perfect moment, he'd like nothing more than to have Dakota to himself and then hold her again as they sat together on the couch. But Sarah was waiting downstairs, and his mom was waiting for all of them. Hooking an arm around Dakota's waist, he led her down the stairs.

"All clear," he said to Sarah as they reached the bottom.

Sarah turned and looked up. "All good?" she asked.

He glanced at Dakota and inclined his head. Yes, this moment was all good. Together, they closed up the shop and climbed into his truck.

A chilly wind blew through the empty street, dropping the temperatures below freezing. Aaron shivered. "I'll have the heat going soon."

Dakota rubbed her hands together quickly and waved to Sarah, who climbed into her own car and pulled away. Aaron had a vision of what his life could be like if only Dakota would stay.

A quiet chuckle came from Dakota. "Thank you. I'd like that."

"Ready to see the sights?" Aaron asked. They sat side by side on the love seat in his mother's living room. Sarah and their mother had left them alone to take care of what remained of lunch. Dakota nodded. Since their discussion earlier, she seemed to be more relaxed with him. Did he dare hope that the change would pave the way for something more? She'd laughed, profusely complimented his mother on her cooking, and teased him along with Sarah.

At times, she would watch them with a wistful expression, sadness stormy in her eyes. Had she contacted her family yet? Was that the reason she seemed so sad, or were there other reasons? Whatever secrets she held, there was only One Who could truly give her the peace she so desperately needed.

"Where are we going?"

"Well, I want to take you to the community center to see what we've been doing, and then I thought we could go take a drive through town to see the light displays. Snowy Springs has some of the best light shows in the whole county."

They said their goodnights to Sarah and his mother and, bundled up in winter coats against the falling snow, got back into his truck to head for the community center.

"What is the matter, Dakota?"

Dakota startled. "You did it again."

"What?"

"You read my mind again."

The thought pleased him. "Why are you sad?"

Dakota shifted her hands to the hem of her coat. "I'm fine."

When he raised his eyebrow in clear disbelief, she sighed and took a deep breath, wiping quickly at her eyes. "Tonight reminded me how much I've lost. Your mom and sister are such lovely people and have been so good to me. I wish I knew how my parents are doing."

"You haven't called them?" He reached over to take her hands. She skittered them away again in full retreat. For all the progress he'd thought they'd made, there was none.

"You don't know what I did to them," she said sadly. And there it was—the secrets she kept to herself. How long would it be before she trusted him?

"You're right—I don't know. But I can tell you that no matter what you've done, I doubt your parents would turn you away or refuse to speak to you if you called them." He took her hands, and this time, she didn't resist. "Look at me, Dakota." His eyes implored her to see what he saw in her. "We've all messed up, but there is nothing we have ever done that can't be forgiven. Whatever it is you've done, you need to forgive yourself. That part isn't up to your parents." Her expression filled with disbelief.

Lord, what can I say to make her see?

He settled back into his seat, hands clenched on the wheel. He released a heavy sigh. "Do you still want to see the lights, or must I take you home?" He glanced over at her, hurt squeezing his chest at her nod.

"The apartment, please."

He didn't miss the fact that she didn't call the apartment her home. She was leaving; he had to remember that. The drive back to the shop was silent. Aaron tried without success to stifle his disappointment. *Lord, help me out here, please. I want to help,* he prayed. He wanted so much for her to trust him and to turn to him, but this was a battle he could not fight for her.

Dakota quietly got out of the truck. Before she could disappear upstairs to her apartment, he was beside her. Taking her slowly in his arms, he hugged her tight and then stepped back. "Whatever you've done is not unforgivable. Phone your folks; talk to them. Maybe then, you will see the same person I see when I look at you. Goodnight."

He gently kissed her cheek and then turned and let himself out of the store. He prayed for her all the way home.

Chapter Twelve

She had to stop doing this to herself. A few days later, Dakota held the phone in her hand again and tried to find the courage to make the call to her parents. She paced up and down the small space in her bedroom, phone flat on her palm. Aaron encouraged her each day to make the call, but somehow, she always found an excuse to avoid it.

Hands trembling, she mustered all her courage and pressed the green button. The call connected in a heartbeat.

"Hello, this is Maureen." Her mother's low alto filled the receiver, and a rush of memories drowned Dakota. The phone fell limply to the floor, and Dakota rushed down to fetch it.

"Hello?" *Come on, brave girl, you can do this.* The voice sounded a lot like Kenny; he'd always been the one to help her see more in herself than she did. Maybe it was Aaron's—she wasn't sure.

"Hi, Mom. It's Dakota," she managed past the hard knot that had somehow climbed from her stomach into her throat and strangled any sound she tried to make. There was silence on the other end, punctuated by what she thought were gasps.

"Mom?" she asked, "are you all right?" Was she dying? Not now, not when she'd finally found the courage to speak to her mom. Dreaded thoughts crowded Dakota's mind, images of her mother gasping for breath all alone. Where was her father?

"Mom, should I call a doctor?"

"Maureen. Maureen? What's the matter, darling?" she heard her father say in the background. He must've been standing beside her mother; his voice was almost as clear as hers.

"Hello, who is this?" her father demanded. She could picture his face—dark eyes wide open; mouth set in a hard, impatient line; face filled with sorrow—the same way he'd looked the day they had bid Kenny goodbye.

"It's me. Dakota," she said softly.

"Dakota?" he said in a husky voice. "Dakota, are you all right? Where are you? Do you need help?"

The hard band of dread weighing down her chest lifted, and the band of tension wound around her chest stretched wide open. For once, she'd done the right thing.

"I'm fine, Dad. Is Mom okay?" she asked.

Her dad quietly chuckled, although she could hear the tears in his voice. "Yes, she's just overcome. She misses you terribly." There was a hardness to his words. She could understand why.

Dakota sank down onto the bed, guilt seeping into her joy. There was still a long road to walk with her parents.

"I'm sorry, Daddy. I don't know how to say how much. I miss you so much, and I'm so sorry." Tears rolled down her face and clogged her voice with emotion.

A long moment of silence followed her apology, and slowly, the dread she'd held earlier returned. Her heart galloped, and a small drop of sweat slid down her cheek. The silence was broken with the murmur of soft voices.

Dakota pressed the phone harder to her ear. She could hear her mother's sobs and her father's low voice soothing her. *This is all my fault.*

A shuffling sound came across the line. "Dakota, are you there?"

"Yes, I'm sorry, Daddy. I'm sorry for hurting you two." The words were far too inadequate to erase the hurt she'd caused. *Dear Lord, please help me.* Would they forgive her after all she'd done? What about the baby?

Another wave of shame sank her further into herself. Nobody knew about the abortion she'd had. Nobody but Bobby. He'd demanded it and then used the guilt and shame to control her. Another wave of self-loathing crashed into her.

"Oh, honey, we'd love to see you. We've missed you, too. We love you."

Relief burst through her fear and self-loathing for a moment. She would have to tell them about their grandchild, but right now, her parents still wanted to see her.

"I-I-I love you, too. Can you forgive me for hurting you and Mom?"

She wanted right now to jump into her car and head for her parents' house, but Aaron needed her here at the store. Christmas was fast approaching, and Aaron spent more time at the community center than he did at the store. He made sure to bring her a cup of coffee in the morning and say goodbye before she closed the store for the night. She'd even saved enough on her earnings to take Mrs. Bouwer up on her offer to rent a room in her house. Her move was the next evening; she hadn't told Aaron yet, but she would.

Dakota didn't like the emptiness of the apartment. Most nights, she felt like a wraith drifting around a cemetery, sad and alone. She loved seeing Aaron, but this was something she needed to do for herself. Aaron would understand.

"Yes, we love you. When can you come?" her dad asked.

Dakota mentally calculated the days to Christmas; it would be difficult but not impossible.

"Can I come the week before Christmas?" She could almost feel their relief across the miles.

"We can't wait to see you." At last, her mother's tear-soaked voice came over the phone, reigniting Dakota's stream again.

"Oh, Mom, I'm so sorry."

"It's okay. Everything will work out as it should." And Dakota believed her.

For the next hour, she and her parents chatted and caught up. The relentless anxiety jumping inside her calmed and then stilled. There was still so much damage to fix, but tonight, she would marvel at the fact that her parents loved her and wanted her back in their lives. She needed to tell Aaron.

"You sound happy," Aaron commented as Dakota tallied consignments and hummed to the song on the radio. The morning had turned out to be a cold one, and Aaron was glad Dakota had stayed indoors. Al had called him earlier to say Dakota's car was almost fixed, and she'd be able to get it back any day now. He hadn't told her yet.

"I called my parents last night," she said.

"You did? That's wonderful. Were they happy to hear from you?"

"Yes, I can't believe it! After everything, they still want to see me. They were happy I called them. They even asked if I could come home for Christmas."

A sudden apprehension gripped Aaron, and he curled his hands along the cold, metal edge of the counter. It needed a polish. Would she be leaving now? "That's good, right?"

Dakota must've missed the anxiety in his words because she continued chatting about her parents and their phone call as if he hadn't spoken.

"Yes, Mom says Christmas would be best with Daddy and his heart . . . "

Had he imagined the growing closeness between the two of them? Was he the only one who could feel the air turn thick whenever they were together? His mind muddled through their times together. Had he imagined it? Did Dakota feel anything for him at all?

"Oh, and Mrs. Bouwer said the room in her house is ready. I'm hoping to move out tonight."

"Move out?" Aaron shouted, tuning back into their conversation. When only silence answered his sudden outburst, Aaron lifted his eyes. Dakota leaned away from the counter, her eyes wide with fright. *Real genius move, Aaron.* What? Oh, yes. Mrs. Bouwer. Dakota had mentioned to him last week that she was thinking of moving into the room at the Bouwer house.

"Sorry, you caught me by surprise. I thought the apartment was all right." Aaron tried his best to smile reassuringly.

The tense set of Dakota's shoulders relaxed. "Well, you know, it's cold, and the store is so empty at night." Her eyes turned to her hands. "It's lonely," she whispered.

"You could come stay with me." The words were out of his mouth before he could stop them. If she was lonely, there was an easy way for her not to be. She could be with him.

Deep color entered Dakota's cheeks. "N-n-no, thank you, Aaron. I appreciate the offer. Mrs. Bouwer's room suits me just fine."

He loved that blush and would miss it when she left. Dakota had made it clear that she was leaving town, and he'd begun to hope that maybe she'd consider staying in Snowy Springs with him.

"Dakota, that came out wrong. I didn't mean move in with me. If you need company, I would be happy to offer myself as company." Dakota's happy expression froze his tongue to his lips. How could he ask her to stay without scaring her into leaving? "And I'm glad you called your folks. What time did you want to move your stuff?"

Her face softened, and his heart pulsed loudly. "Aaron, I would love your company. After work?" She tenderly wrapped her hands around his. He drew her down the length of the counter and around the edge. He wanted her in his arms so badly, he ached with the thought. Dakota smiled and stepped closer until the heat of her body pulsed beside his. She held his wrists, guiding his arms around her waist. Aaron closed the last inch, bringing her firmly into his chest. Her heart pounded beside his.

"Dakota," he growled. With solicitude, he buried his face into her soft, flowing hair and drank in her scent.

"Yes," she said breathlessly. His pulse skyrocketed as Dakota melted against him.

"Thank you, Aaron, for encouraging me. I owe you."

Aaron chuckled into her neck. She smelled wonderful this close. "You don't owe me. You had the courage to make the call. I just gave you the nudge you needed."

"Yes, but still," she said, leaning away from him.

Aaron lifted his head, confused. "Are you okay?"

Smiling, Dakota slid her hands up his arms and curled them around his neck, tunneling her fingers into the short, black strands of his hair. If she kept doing that, he was going to break the promise he'd made to himself and kiss her.

"Yes."

Their gazes caught and held; those lips he'd thought about kissing more times than he could count were just out of reach. He swallowed hard, pushing down the temptation to taste them. Dakota had been hurt in ways he couldn't imagine. It made him angry when he'd thought of her being at the hands of a man who did not show her worth. Yet, here she was in his arms. Open and trusting.

Carefully, he inched closer until he could feel her rapid breaths on his own lips. "Dakota, I don't know how much longer I can stop myself from kissing you." He groaned.

A low chuckle whispered against his mouth as Dakota crossed the last inch and pressed her velvety lips against his. Lightly, hesitantly, and then his brain short-circuited.

Chapter Thirteen

The kiss came to an abrupt halt as the glass door of the store smacked into the stack of garden accessories beside it. Forks, shovels, and a few pruning sheers clattered with a loud crash to the floor. Dakota jumped away from Aaron and stared in horror as Bobby filled the entrance.

"So, this is where you've been hiding?" he asked. The arrogant sneer on his angry features spoke of what he would do to her if he had caught her alone.

Dakota cringed behind Aaron. This couldn't be happening.

"Can I help you?" Aaron asked, drawing to his full height, his broad shoulders stiff and straight.

His dark eyes that had looked so tenderly at her a moment ago shone with just barely suppressed anger. She could feel it radiating off him. Bobby laughed and said something coarse. Color flooded Dakota's cheeks.

"No, I can see what I came for. Dakota, get your stuff. We need to leave now."

Before she could stop herself, she'd turned to respond, just like she'd always done. He'd found her—just like she knew he would. When it came to things he thought he owned, Bobby was as jealous as they came.

Aaron's callused hand gently encircled her wrist, stopping her. "You don't have to do what he says. You can make up your own mind." Aaron's voice was rough with some emotion, but when she looked up, there was only tenderness.

"Ah, you've managed to convince this poor sap that you like him. Well, let me tell you something about this girl." She couldn't let this go on.

"Stop it, Bobby. I'll get my things. You just wait outside." Victorious arrogance shone on the face that she'd thought would be the answer to the loneliness that had filled her life since Kenny had died. But as soon as Bobby knew he'd had her, the monster had emerged.

She loosened her hand from Aaron's with a shudder and wrapped her hands around her stomach. It had been a good dream while it lasted, but reality always came in. She should've known that nothing this good could last forever. Not for her. Guilt and shame fought for dominance; the weight settled like a noose around her neck.

"Look, I don't know who you are or who you think you are; but Dakota is my employee, and I have her under contract to stay here until Christmas."

What was he doing? Why was he standing up for her?

Bobby's face flushed dangerously—a dark, menacing light burned in his evil eyes. Fear stabbed her chest; anxiety ripped through her lungs; and she stumbled over her feet before crashing to the floor. Bobby's savage laughter rang out. "You stupid girl, can't you even walk up the stairs the right way? That's your idiotic way, isn't it, Dakota? Can't do anything simple asked of you."

Footsteps walked closer to her. She curled herself into a ball, hoping to deflect the blows.

"Dakota, here, let me help you up." Aaron slowly pulled her to her feet and gave her an encouraging smile. Immediately, his smile made her braver. She worried what Aaron would say if he knew about her past, but no matter what Bobby said, she was going nowhere with him.

Bobby, having contained himself, tapped his foot irritably. "Well, hurry up."

Squeezing Aaron's hand, she let go and stood up straight. It was time to be brave. If what the pastor had said was true, a whole host of angels stood with her. "I'm not going with you, Bobby, and there is nothing you can do or say to make me."

Dark anger once again encompassed his face; and he lunged toward her, arm stretched out, fist clenched. He didn't even get close to her. With a sickening crunch, Aaron's fist met Bobby's cheek, stopping his forward motion with an undeniable suddenness. Bobby crashed onto the floor, howling with profanities.

"Dakota, call the sheriff," Aaron said as he took a protective stance in front of her.

Hands shaking, she lifted the phone to her ear.

"Hello, can I please speak to the sheriff? We have a problem at Aaron's store."

His muscles ached with anger and tension—so much so that he could feel the pain of his nails pressing into the soft flesh of his hands. Who did this monster think he was, coming in here and demanding anything from Dakota? Was this the man who had beat her, whose scars she wore the day she came to town? Bobby jumped to his feet and glared at Aaron.

"Why are you defending that piece of rubbish behind you?"

"Because she's not rubbish, and she deserves far more than a scumbag like you."

If it were possible for rage to be a color, Aaron would say it was a dark reddish purple. Bobby's face took on the hue as he lunged for Aaron. He wasn't particularly big, but Aaron knew the type—the type that fought dirty and beat women. A meaty fist flew at his face, and he easily blocked it before it could connect with his jaw. Another came quickly from the other side, and he tried to deflect it by raising his arm across his face. The fist crashed into his forearm and bounced into his chin. Pain burst into stars behind his eyelids.

Again, Bobby came for him, this time low in the waist. Bobby bent low and drove himself into Aaron's stomach. Aaron bent over and gripped him in a bear hug around the waist. He yanked Bobby up, effectively winding him before driving a hard elbow into his back. Bobby howled again, and more profanities spewed from his bloody mouth. He had a filthy mouth. What had Dakota seen in this guy? It didn't matter. She wouldn't deal with him alone.

Bobby crumbled to the floor, his head hitting a wooden kitchen step with a decisive thud. He rolled over and lay still. For a bit, Aaron watched, hands on his knees, the excuse for a human being laying on his store floor. Sickness crawled over his stomach as he thought of his sweet Dakota in the hands of this monster. Was this the kind of man she liked? He immediately refuted his own thoughts. Fear rolled off Dakota. This was one of the mistakes she had made.

Straightening, he moved closer to Dakota. She cringed in the corner between the drills. Her face was pale, her body stiff. She shook periodically, but as soon as she did, she stiffened her spine and held tighter to the long wood axe in her hands.

"Dakota," Aaron said softly, afraid she'd pass out on him, "it's okay. He's out. He won't hurt you again."

She wobbled, her face becoming dangerously pale. The axe fell from her limp hand with a clatter. It was too much for Aaron. Instantly, he was beside her, enfolding her shaking form into his tired arms. He didn't care about her past only her future. He desperately hoped he'd have a place in it. He breathed in time with her breath until they slowed, and he silently thanked God that Dakota hadn't been at the store alone today. Who knew what Bobby would've done to her?

"Are you all right?" he asked, holding her tighter. The idea of giving her space anytime soon fought against his very nature as a man in love. *Love.* The word rolled around like a gobstopper in his mouth. He savored the sweetness as it became part of his very being. He was in love with Dakota—wholly, fully, and with everything in him.

The door clattered open again, and Aaron stiffened. He grabbed Dakota by the hand and hurried out from the aisle where she'd hidden. Bobby lay where he'd left him but was starting to come around. Sheriff Donaldson and his deputies spilled into the shop in a wild flurry of shouts and stamping feet.

"You all right?" he asked Aaron and nodded to Dakota.

"We're okay, thanks. That man's name is Bobby. He threatened Dakota and tried to force her to go with him."

Deputy Paulson hauled Bobby to his feet. Bobby growled and said something under his breath. "There'll be no need to say those words in front of a lady," the deputy said.

"Lady? I don't see a lady."

Aaron stifled the urge to knock Bobby out again.

Deputy Paulson paused. "I can if you want," he said.

Aaron grinned. "Nah, I think that shiner should remind him to pick on someone his own size."

With a hearty laugh, the deputy dragged Bobby's uncooperative form into the squad car.

Sheriff Donaldson took out a small notebook. "Do you want to press charges?"

"Absolutely."

"No," Dakota said at the same time. Her face was still pale, and her body shook so hard that he could feel his teeth jarring in his gums. "I just want him away from me."

"That can be arranged. We'll be sure to run him out of town—as soon as he is able to stand by himself, that is." The sheriff collected the rest of the deputies, and they filed out into waiting squad cars, leaving Aaron and Dakota alone once again.

"Come, let's get you some hot chocolate," Aaron said, leading Dakota, molded to his side, up to her apartment. She sat comatose at the kitchen table, her eyes red and empty, her eyelids fluttering as if she needed sleep.

"Do you want to lie down?" he asked. Hot water joined hot chocolate powder in the mugs followed by cream and marshmallows, and still, Dakota said nothing.

Aaron handed her the mug, and she took a few quick sips. "I'm sorry you had to see that," she said.

Chapter Fourteen

There was no use in lying or keeping anything back. Bobby had effectively destroyed any hope of her keeping their ugly past from Aaron. The sweetness in the hot chocolate lifted the relentless fatigue that gathered in her limbs. Aaron sat quietly beside her, his expression thoughtful as he waited for her.

She loved this man so much. The moment her lips had touched Aaron's, she'd known what her heart had been trying to tell her and her head had been denying. Aaron was not like Bobby. She'd finally realized that tonight. He wouldn't hurt her, and he would treat her properly. But because he was not like Bobby, he could never be with a woman like her.

"I met Bobby a year after Kenny died. My parents struggled to come to terms with Kenny's death and seemed oblivious to the pain I was in. I felt left out and unloved, as if my parents had lost their capacity to love me when Kenny died. I know differently now." How she wished she had listened to their pleading, their advice that Bobby was no good.

"Anyway, Bobby was everything a rebellious teenage girl needed to leave her parents. The day I graduated high school, we skipped town. I would like to say that he suddenly changed, but that would be untrue. I knew he was dangerous, and it was part of his charm."

A long breath emptied her lungs. She'd been such a fool. Young and stupid, she hadn't heard her parents' concerns or the stories around town.

"Two years ago, I became pregnant. I was terrified. Bobby had made no secret of the fact that he didn't want children. He'd gone as far as telling me that if I ever got pregnant, he'd kill the baby himself."

Bile rose from her stomach as she remembered the conversation. She'd thought he'd kill her that day. "I was on my way home when Bobby surprised me. He saw the bag from the drugstore in my hand and knew immediately. I don't know how he knew." She cringed; the words and blows echoed around her. She clenched her hands tighter around the mug, trying to squash the memories that surged to the surface of her mind. The beating she took that night was amongst the worst she'd experienced at Bobby's hands as if he wanted to permanently make sure she could not make the same mistake again.

Tears spilled from her eyes, and Aaron leaned forward to wipe them away. She moved away from his touch, opting for a tissue instead. "When it was done, I cried for a week and told myself I would leave him so that he could never do something like that to me again. But Bobby came with flowers and chocolates and said how sorry he was." And like the cliché battered woman, she'd accepted. She should've known better, even then. But she'd held onto the hope that somehow the experience had changed him.

"The night I left, Bobby and I had a big fight. He was drunk again and in the mood to use me as a punching bag." She'd planned for weeks to leave, squirreling her stuff into the apartment storage room a little at a time until the opening came and she left. That night,

Bobby had done her a favor by passing out. She'd known he'd be dead to the world until morning.

"The bruises at the hospital," Aaron said. He again reached for her, and again, she pushed him away. He was just being nice. How could he want to touch her after all she'd said?

"To this day, I don't know how I knew I needed to leave. It was a feeling of foreboding that wouldn't seem to leave me. It kept on for weeks. After he beat me and passed out, the feeling intensified, and I knew it was time to run."

"God was speaking to you."

"Maybe. The pastor said He is always with me. I guess I didn't really believe that until this very moment. I shudder to think what would've happened if he'd found me alone." She swallowed hard, fighting for composure against her tears. Aaron hesitantly stood to his feet. He opened his arms to her waiting, accepting. The struggle overwhelmed her, and she gave into the desire to be in his arms because anything else hurt too much. Relaxing into his chest, she let herself dream and wish. After all, there was no harm in wishes. For now, she'd allow Aaron to hold her; and tomorrow, she'd be back with her parents.

Something was off with Dakota. She was too quiet. After spilling her history, she sat silent in his arms. Her hands continued to move busily in her lap, and the light that had been in her eyes when he'd kissed her had died. The same fearful emptiness he'd seen when they'd met had made a reappearance.

Another shudder racked her body; his arms tightened in response. Dakota melted just for a moment into his chest and then gently pushed him back. "I think I need a long soak and some sleep," she said. There was a hollowness to her tone like all the life had drained from her. His heart clenched in sympathy. What did this mean for him? For them?

He swallowed down his panic. Dakota was in shock—that was as clear as day. Maybe he should ask to sleep on the couch tonight to make sure that if her sleep was riddled with nightmares, he would be there to hold her. Although, based on how she now held herself away from him, he knew his offer would be rejected.

Lovingly lifting up her chin, Aaron searched deeply into her sad eyes. "I love you," he said. "No matter what happened tonight, I mean it."

Dakota merely nodded. "I'll see you in the morning," she said, confirming what he'd already thought. She needed space, and he needed to give it to her despite the unease resting in his chest like a deadweight.

Standing, he pulled Dakota up with him and kissed her forehead. "In the morning, then. I'll let myself out."

He turned her toward him and waited until she stepped into his arms. He hugged her close, his unease releasing its grip on him. Dakota sighed and, for an instant, held him tighter.

As they parted, Dakota said, "Sleep tight, Aaron. Thank you for standing up for me and defending me from Bobby."

"I love you, Dakota. I could do no less."

His words meant something to her. He could see it in the way her dull eyes warmed slightly.

But "Good night" was all she said.

Fear once again gripped his chest because her good night sounded a lot like goodbye. Would this be the end of them? *Lord, help her. Help her to see how much I love her and how much her past doesn't matter to me.*

Once he had climbed into the cab of his truck, he allowed himself to give into his own emotions. When Bobby had lunged for Dakota, Aaron had known he never wanted to be without her again. In that instant, he could see a future with her, one he desperately wanted. If she would let him, he would do anything in his power to make her happy.

His house was quiet and empty when he walked through the door. He looked around the living room, imagining what it would be like to live with Dakota as husband and wife. Her penchant for weak coffee and her need for a limitless supply of gummy sweets only made her dearer to him.

The emotional rollercoaster he'd been on tonight had exhausted him, and food held no particular appeal. He made a grilled cheese sandwich, anyway, and swallowed it down in two bites. Restless, he turned on the shower and washed the day's grime and Bobby's filth off his hands and body.

His thoughts dwelled on Dakota. Was she okay? Was she having nightmares? He was sure she was, but if he'd insisted on staying, he was sure she'd have found a way to reject him. It hurt—he wouldn't lie—but after seeing the abuse Bobby had piled on her, he'd held his peace.

The night faded gradually into morning as he lay tossing and turning in his bed. Before the sun had fully risen, he was out of bed and on his way back to the store. Back to Dakota.

"Dakota," he called as he opened the door. After last night, she was likely to spook for any reason. Only silence greeted him. The store lights were off, but then again, Dakota probably wasn't up yet. He took the stairs up to the apartment two at a time and came to a halt. One light burned in the kitchen, and the rest of the apartment was empty. Maybe she'd moved out on her own after he'd left, unable to stay in the apartment after what happened. His phone beeped in his pocket, and he drew it out to call the Bouwer house. There was one text message waiting.

I'm sorry. He didn't need a name or a number to know it came from Dakota. Rushing out of the store, he gunned the truck to Al's. Dakota couldn't have gone far. Al still had her car.

Slamming the brakes, Aaron came to a screeching stop outside Al's shop and jumped out of the truck, just about taking the door with him. Al opened the entryway in his coverall, no coat. Al rarely wore a coat. It had to be thirty-five below for Al to get cold.

"What can I do for you this early in the morning, Aaron?"

"Is Dakota here?" he asked urgently.

Al shook his head. "She called last night and said she needed her car to go see her parents and wanted to know if it was ready. I told her it was, and she came by to collect it right after. What's the matter?"

"She's gone." The words felt like a blow to his gut, and he gasped for a breath. "She's left town."

Al's confused eyes met his. "She said since the beginning that she was only stopping through. I assumed you knew about her leaving town."

God, how could You let this happen? "No, I didn't know she planned to leave." Why hadn't he insisted on staying with her last night?

Maybe then, he could have convinced her to stay, assure her of how much he loved her.

Turning back to his truck, Aaron climbed in and stared without seeing down the long, lonely road from Al's shop to town. Tears pooled in his eyes, and he blinked them back. Once again, a woman he loved had left town without explanation, and there was nothing he could do about it.

Chapter Fifteen

"Dakota?" A wary looking woman Dakota had, up until five years ago, called Mom, slowly walked down the stained wooden stairs of the bungalow Dakota had been staring at for the better part of an hour. Her mother paused, her shaking hands raised to cover her mouth. "Dakota, is that you?"

Sucking up her courage, Dakota pushed open the car door, closed it, and froze. Emotions like a hurricane thrashed through her at the sight of her mom and dad. She stumbled forward toward them. "I'm sorry," she said. "I'm so sorry."

A soft pair of arms surrounded by an equally firm pair enfolded her, and she sank into them, rivulets of tears streaming down her face. "I'm so sorry."

"Oh, baby," her mother said, taking Dakota's face between her palms. "Let's go inside and talk."

Throat tight, Dakota nodded.

The house was exactly the way she remembered it. The same set of brown leather couches sat in the front room just beyond the door. The same black coffee tables stood at their arms. The white gossamer curtains still hung in the bay windows; they had been a wedding gift to her parents from her gran. Pictures of her and Kenny in various stages of growing crowded the white walls. The only thing that was different in her memory was the flat screen TV on the north wall.

Everywhere she looked, memories swept past her eyes. She and Kenny playing hide-and-seek and accidentally knocking over her mother's prize vase. Dakota and Kenny smiling as they posed for photos at her sophomore spring dance. On and on, the memories went. She blinked, holding back her tears and moved deeper into the room. Her parents sat down as they always had in the love seat in front of the window. She took the single sofa opposite them, nervously sliding the hem of her gray sweatshirt between her fingers.

"I'm sorry," she said again.

Her mother nodded. "Whatever the reason that you left Dakota, please know that we never stopped loving you."

She could see it now—the love her parents had for her. She could see how much her running away had affected them. A part of her wished she could go back in time, sit down with her parents, and talk. Maybe then, none of the choices she'd made since that day would have come to pass. *Regret was a tough but fair teacher.* She remembered reading the quote somewhere. Guilt would not change the past; regret would not detract the choices she'd made; but the grace she'd accepted would allow her to make things right where she'd done so much wrong. Pain and peace intermingled. She rose from her seat and knelt before her parents, taking one of each of their hands in hers.

"I missed you so much."

As one, her parents leaned forward and wrapped their free arms around her shoulders, drawing her into their warm huddle.

"All is forgiven," her father whispered hoarsely. "We are just so glad you came home."

A sense of homecoming overcame her as her eyes filled with tears. A piece of her heart that belonged to her family was set back in place. She smiled as she remembered her brother, his mischievous blue eyes and blond hair, much like her own, and his smile; she could see it in her father. *Thank You, Lord,* she thought. One pain had lifted, but there was another. It was so much deeper. She would carry it for the rest of her life—her love for Aaron Bakker.

The rain was miserable. But she supposed miserable was to be her new state of being. Another flurry of snowflakes raced to the ground. Large drops of wet mush slid down the window and dumped unceremoniously into her mother's plants. A pity—they were nice plants.

If someone looked at her, they would just see a woman with a sad face staring out into the rain, but the drops that slid down the clear pane covered the drops that continued to run from her eyes. Pain wasn't an unfamiliar emotion to her. With Bobby, she'd experienced all kinds of pain. But this pain drove her to her knees until she didn't have the strength to stand up again.

More rain fell, and Dakota sighed. Aaron's sad eyes stared back at her behind her eyelids when she blinked. Would she ever forget him? Would she ever move past the pain? She doubted it. For the second time in her life, she knew the price of her stubbornness.

When she'd left home to run after Bobby, she'd missed her parents, and she couldn't thank God enough that they were now back in her life. But what she'd found with Aaron was something irreplaceable.

Her phone buzzed quietly beside her, but she let it go to voicemail. The strength to answer had left her. She'd known what Aaron would say the moment he opened his mouth, and yet when the words were out, a desperate fear had surfaced.

She loved Aaron—there was no doubt about it. She loved him fully, wholly, and whichever other way a woman could love a man. But why had she run? She wasn't good enough for a man like Aaron. She wasn't clean and pure; she'd done things and . . .

Dakota crumpled down onto the bed and cradled her head in her hands. And she was afraid. She was so afraid he would look at her one day with the same disappointment and disgust as Bobby had. What if she did something to make him lose his love for her?

She picked up the phone and dialed her mother's number. "Hey, Mom," she said softly, her voice garbled by her tears.

"Dakota? Are you okay?"

"Yes, no. I don't know. I blew it, Mom." Spectacularly was too small a word to say how she'd blown her chances with Aaron.

"What are you talking about?"

"With Aaron. Mom, I blew it."

"I'll be up in a minute."

"You're in the house? I thought you were at Aunt Maggie's."

"I was, but something just told me I needed to come home."

It was God. Despite her dark mood, Dakota smiled. From the time she'd made the commitment in church two weeks ago, peace had permeated every part of her life. Bobby was gone, and because of her choice, so was Aaron.

God, what do I do? Can I trust him to love me the way You do? The peace inside her expanded slowly, filling the last of the cracks in her heart. God was smiling on her, and like a Father, He whispered, *Trust Me. You are clean. You are forgiven. Trust Me.*

The sorrowful storm she'd carried over the last few days broke open. Warm sunlight and a color wheel of hues shone in her mind's eye. She was loved, and she was forgiven. She could trust God in all things, even in her love for Aaron and his love for her. They would be okay.

A soft knock came from the doorway. "Dakota?" Her mother's eyes went wide at her tears. "Oh, honey. Are you okay?"

"Yes, Mom, I think I finally am."

The deep frown between her mother's eyebrows smoothed out. "Want to talk about it?"

"Mom, I'm sorry to miss Christmas again with you and Dad, but I need to go back to Snowy Springs. I need to tell Aaron I love him."

Her mother's smile was brilliant. "Then go. I know your heart has been there. I was just waiting for your heart to catch up with your head. You always were a stubborn one."

Dakota chuckled. "I must be more like Daddy than I thought."

"You have no idea," her mother said with a hearty laugh.

"Go after her. She's at her mom's."

The hammer hung in midair. "How do you know that, squirt?"

Sarah shrugged her small shoulders. "She called me. She's my friend, too, and I miss her. And it couldn't be clearer than if you had a sign posted on your forehead that you're miserable without her."

"She doesn't want me." Aaron blew out a heavy breath, and the hammer dropped onto the roof struts beside him heavily.

"I happen to have it on good authority that she's as miserable as you are."

That was news to him. A spark of happiness caught up in his heart—not because Dakota was miserable but because she was missing him. "I can't just go there. They don't know me from Adam, and I doubt I would be invited."

"You're not afraid that she doesn't want to see you but that her dad won't like you?" Sarah asked, her face alight and teasing.

"Now, hang on, I'm pretty sure she doesn't want to see me."

The teasing light faded. Sarah's face softened with compassion. "Aaron, go after her. Isn't she worth the risk?"

Dakota was more worth it than he could say. The risk was minimal when it came to her because his heart would never be complete; his life would be a half-life without her.

The snow slowly trailed down the window of the shop, the dim light from the gray afternoon reminding him of the color of Dakota's eyes. She would always be worth the risk of his pride and possible rejection. She would still be worth it, even if he had to walk to the other side of the world to find her.

A rightness that had eluded him since the day Dakota had driven away sealed the bleeding in his chest.

"It looks like I'm going to find my girl."

"You go get her." Sarah handed over his keys. "I think you need to shower, though. This been-in-the-woodshed-all-day look is not going to work."

Aaron laughed.

Chapter Sixteen

A heavy wind yanked the shop door from his hand as the gust of wind blew him and about a foot of snow into the room. Aaron stamped his boots and threw his coat and gloves on the nearby counter. There was so much to do.

Dakota's smell was in the air—from the front desk, to the coat rack, and all around. When had it become so potent? Was it because he missed her so much that the smell seemed stronger today? Taking a deep inhale, he grabbed the last few invoices for the community center rebuild and moved them with his laptop to the bag.

The fresh, floral smell of Dakota called to him again. If he closed his eyes, he could imagine her soft arms surrounding him when he held her close. Groaning, he pressed his eyes closed for a moment and ran his hand through his messy hair. Man, he must be losing it; he could swear she was right in front of him.

Sliding the laptop into the bag in exasperation, followed by the invoices, he quickly cleared up the work area. He needed the place to be clean. Sarah said she'd watch it for a few days while Aaron planned to be away. He circled the counter, focused on the checkout scanner, and quickly tallied the day's takings.

A small sound made him pause his hand. His eyes darted around the room and then froze on a lone female figure that stood at the edge of the stairs. Her blonde hair shone with an ethereal glow, her gray eyes filled with a timid hope. She smiled anxiously, lifting her hand to wave.

"Dakota?" he asked, his voice squeezing past the lump in his throat.

"Hi, Aaron," Dakota said. Her nervousness was clear by the tangle of her fingers.

Her eyes trailed down to her hands, and he hurried out from behind the counter up to her. He couldn't lose sight of those eyes, not when he'd missed them so much. After a moment's hesitation, he lifted her chin, hoping she wouldn't vanish if he touched her.

"Dakota," he whispered. Her face lifted, tenderness pooling her gaze into liquid. His heart hammered as he stepped closer, the heat of her body warming his.

"What are you doing here?" he asked at last. "I was just . . . never mind. What are you doing back in town? Is something wrong?" He didn't care why she was back, only that she was.

Color washed into her soft cheeks, and her skin called to him. He remembered the soft feel of her cheeks under his thumbs when he'd kissed her.

"I'm sorry I left. I came back to tell you something I should have told you long ago," she said softly.

She smiled in a way he hadn't seen before; his pulse leapt with hope. Had she come to tell him she loved him? That she'd missed him as much as he'd missed her? That she desperately wanted to be in his life as much as he wanted to be in hers?

Noting her shyness, he tentatively took her hands in his and drew her over to the place where they'd often drunk their morning coffee before opening the store to customers. He pulled the café-style chairs closer together. Any distance away from her was unbearable. Dakota's eyes shone with amusement.

"What?" he asked.

A gentle smile was her only response as she entangled their hands and brought them to rest on the table. "When I left Bobby, I swore to myself that I was done with men and done with love. I would never be put in a place where someone had the power to hurt me the way he had. I made many mistakes, mistakes I regret." She sighed. "God has forgiven me, and with time, I hope to forgive myself." She moved closer to him, her gaze fixed to his. There was hope there, and there was fear—not fear of him but fear of his rejection.

With their entangled hands, he lifted her from her seat and into his lap. Dakota chuckled as she curled into him.

"I love you, Aaron Bakker. The past is behind me, and I want more than anything to experience the future with you. If you'll have me, I want to wake up each morning with you by my side. I want to climb mountains and go swimming in the lake. I want to have the craziness of this snowy winter." She paused. "I still struggle to trust at times, but I've been speaking to the pastor at my parents' church. With time and the grace of God, I will be better at it."

There was so much hope in her expression mixed with a pleading to understand. He did understand. Everyone made mistakes. He doubted there was a person alive who didn't have regrets of some kind or another, and everyone had a past.

Unable to speak, he pulled Dakota to her feet and into his chest, wrapping his arms around her. Dakota's gorgeous eyes glimmered, and he found himself falling into them in the same way he had that first day in the hospital. His heart had known long before his brain had caught up with it that he would love Dakota until the end of his days. Cupping her cheek in his hand, he lowered his head toward her until there was nothing but a breath of air between them.

"And I love you, Dakota Manning, and I will love you forever. I promise, with the help of God, to love you well for as long as this life allows me."

Dakota's small arms met at his back, and she pressed herself closer. Her pouty, pink mouth lifted closer to his until only an inch remained. He closed the space and brushed her lips gently, once, again, and again, savoring the feel of her lips against his. At last, he pressed his mouth firmly to hers, coaxing, loving, persuading. The kiss deepened. Silence hung over the store as they kissed. He snuggled Dakota to his chest. "In case that didn't tell you how much I missed you, you could phone Sarah and ask how miserable I've been without you."

"I missed you, too."

Delight, happiness, joy, and attraction crashed together in a grand symphony. The wild pumping of her heart beat in time with the thump of the chest pressed close to her. How she loved this man. How had she thought she would ever be the best person she could be without him? How had she thought that losing him had been a viable choice?

None of that mattered now. She was here in Aaron's arms—the love he'd professed for her clear in every beat of his heart, every breath that he breathed, and every sweep of his mouth. How had she thought that she could live without him? Without this?

Aaron groaned softly against her mouth, and she felt herself smile. When they parted, those brown eyes she would love for a lifetime smiled down at her.

"I love you," he said again. She rested her head on his chest right over his thumping heart. The past was in the past, and now, the only thing they had to look forward to was the future. Joy burst like the opening of a flower, and she shivered from the emotion of it.

Aaron pulled her closer, if that were possible, and she listened as his rapid heart rate slowed until it thudded with a reliable beat. God had brought Aaron into her life when her days and nights had been a constant blur of darkness. And now, at last, the light was brighter.

"As much as I'd like to continue this, there is somewhere important I need to be . . . " Aaron said. His eyes danced with the teasing she loved so much.

"Oh, where are you going?" She tried to step back, but Aaron held her fast.

"Well, apparently, there is this girl that I seem to have fallen in love with waiting for me at her mother's house."

Dakota tipped her head to the side as understanding slowly dawned. "You were coming to get me?" she asked. Another shiver of delight raced down her spine.

"Anytime, anywhere. The world would not have been big enough to keep me from you," he said against her mouth before kissing her again. The kiss was soft, and a warm glow spread from her heart to the tips of her fingers and ends of her toes. How could she be this blessed?

"I'm sorry for leaving, Aaron," she said when they eventually parted. "I was angry and ashamed, and I didn't believe that a man like you could ever love someone like me. I know God loves me and has washed me clean, but how could you love me after all I've done? And how could I ever compete with someone like Lacey?"

Aaron's finger rested gently on her lips. "I love you—past, future, and everything. There is nothing to forgive. Let's leave Lacey and Bobby in the past where they belong and embrace the future God has given us."

His words sealed the one remaining crack in her heart, and it beat for the first time whole and healed. "I'd like that."

A light buzzing interrupted the moment, and Aaron chuckled as she pulled her phone from her back pocket. "Let me guess—my sister?" Aaron asked.

Dakota nodded. "How did she know?"

"Oh, you know Sarah."

"Yes, I do," she said with a laugh. "I do indeed."

Epilogue

Aaron covered a smile as Michael walked into his mother's living room and right up to Sarah. The past few months since Michael's return to Snowy Springs had been filled with ups and downs, but at least during the turmoil, one thing had become abundantly clear to any who had eyes to see. Michael was head over heels in love with Sarah, and Sarah, despite her protests, felt the same. Aaron might have been furious with his best friend if not for the emotions he saw bouncing between the two whenever they were in the same space. Curling his arm around Dakota's waist, he pulled her into his side and to the fireplace.

"They'll work it out. You'll see," she said softly. "Like we had to."

Aaron nodded. His heart ached for his friend and sister; they had their own battles to fight and their own demons to face. He bent to kiss Dakota, revelling in the soft texture of her lips. He pulled away. "I know. I wish I knew how to help."

Dakota chuckled softly and kissed him again. "I know that big brother is in there roaring, but this is one you can't fight for either of them—as much as you want to."

She handed him a short piece of kindling. "Now, please show me how to light this thing," she said, gesturing to the unlit fireplace.

Aaron pulled his eyes away just in time to see Sarah duck out the back door of his mother's house and Michael follow closely behind.

Dakota was right. Taking the flint from Dakota, he struck a match, lit it, and bent to light the other logs in the fireplace. Once the fire was blazing, he pulled Dakota to a nearby sofa and sat down with her in his arms. They watched the fire as it popped and blazed.

He caught his mother's gaze as she crossed the open doorway. She nodded to the outside, a smile on her face. He sat up, unsettling Dakota from his chest in time to hear the sound of happiness spilling from outside the door. In a flash, he was on his feet, dragging Dakota with him.

"I assume she said yes?"

Michael nodded, a beaming Sarah nestled into his side. Finally. God had brought both him and Sarah happiness at a time when they'd least expected it. Dakota laid her palm against his beating heart as they watched Michael produce a ring from his pocket and put it on Sarah's hand. He gazed down into Dakota's eyes; it wasn't time for them yet but soon.

Silently, he bent down, sealing the promise with a kiss.

The End

Coming Next From Michelle Dykman

Redeeming Antiquity

After Megan Davis walks away from her marriage to Noah Thomas, she throws all her time and energy into becoming one of the most renowned archeologists in her field. So when her father, the indomitable General Samuel Davis, requests her help to retrieve a lost artifact from Europe, she grabs on with both hands.

The last six years have been tough for Noah Thomas. First, his wife leaves him, and then his unit is attacked, forcing him into months of recovery. After his brother, Michael, returns from being held as a prisoner of war, he questions his future with the armed forces. Before he can decide, he is presented with a new assignment—security detail for an expedition to Italy.

What should have been a quick in and out with the artifact becomes a task that will surpass any Noah has faced while in the army. And when Megan goes missing, it is up to Noah to put aside their painful past and follow the clues to find her.

For more information about
Michelle Dykman
&
The Deal with Dakota
please visit:

www.michelledykman.com

Ambassador International's mission is to magnify the Lord Jesus Christ and promote His Gospel through the written word.

We believe through the publication of Christian literature, Jesus Christ and His Word will be exalted, believers will be strengthened in their walk with Him, and the lost will be directed to Jesus Christ as the only way of salvation.

For more information about
AMBASSADOR INTERNATIONAL
please visit:

www.ambassador-international.com

Thank you for reading this book. Please consider leaving us a review on your favorite retailer's website, Goodreads or Bookbub, or our website.

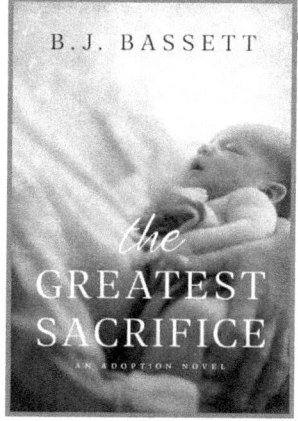

B.J. BASSETT

the GREATEST SACRIFICE

AN ADOPTION NOVEL

Stevie is a typical teenager of the sixties. But when her dad dies, she and her mom find themselves living a life they never expected.

Annie has it all—a loving husband, money, and a beautiful home. But all she has ever wanted is to be a mother.

Two women find themselves on two separate journeys to make the greatest sacrifice for the child they love. But can love truly conquer all? Or will the greatest sacrifice be too much?

Niamh is a devout Catholic living with her parents in Ireland in 1908. She has never doubted their faith, but when she joins a suffragist movement, Niamh suddenly finds herself being introduced to women from who all believe that women deserve to be treated as well as men. As Niamh begins to imagine a world where women and men are equal, she meets Fred, the brother of one of her sister suffragists. Based on a true story, The Last Letter is a tale of overcoming prejudice and finding love against all odds.

THE LAST LETTER

BETHAN MARSHALL

A NOVEL

WHO BROUGHT THE DOG TO CHURCH?

a novel

TRACY L. SMOAK

Betty is sure that Ida Lou does not belong in their church when the woman shows up to the Good Friday service with her small dog in tow. But before she knows what's happening, Betty—along with the other women of the WUFHs (Women United For Him)—is pushed into helping the woman. God works in mysterious ways—and through ordinary people. The town of Prosper is about to experience some drama—and it all starts with a dog who comes to church.

www.ingramcontent.com/pod-product-compliance
Lightning Source LLC
Chambersburg PA
CBHW060427260626
47161CB00005B/1819